"I intend both ... baby, and ke...

Adam stared down at her, his eyes oddly blank. "I see. It's ultimatum time." He shrugged. "All right. You leave me with no choice. We get married."

"Oh, *please*," she said scathingly. "Right from the beginning you made it clear that marriage and a family are the last things you want. Besides, shotgun weddings are a bit out-of-date, Adam. Please don't trouble yourself. I'll manage on my own."

Adam's mouth tightened. "You're being stupid again, Lowri. There's nothing else for it. I'll arrange a quiet wedding as quickly as possible."

Dear Reader,

A special delivery—our bouncing baby series. Every month we've been bringing you your very own bundle of joy—a cute and delightful romance by one of your favorite authors. This series is all about the true labor of love—parenthood and how to survive it! Because, as our heroes and heroines have been discovering, two's company and three (or four…or five) is a family!

This month, with the last arrival in our series, comes a triple (or should that be triplet) helping of pleasure—a baby, a miracle for Christmas *and* a new story set in Pennington, Catherine George's delightful English town.

Season's Greetings!

The Editors
Harlequin Romance

Reform of
the Rake
Catherine George

Harlequin Books

TORONTO • NEW YORK • LONDON
AMSTERDAM • PARIS • SYDNEY • HAMBURG
STOCKHOLM • ATHENS • TOKYO • MILAN
MADRID • WARSAW • BUDAPEST • AUCKLAND

ISBN 0-373-03484-9

REFORM OF THE RAKE

First North American Publication 1997.

CHAPTER ONE

Lowri gave her distinguished, grey-haired male customer a friendly, courteous smile, her amusement well hidden as she gift-wrapped expensive scraps of sexy underwear so very obviously intended for someone other than his wife. When he'd gone she exchanged a grin with her nearest colleague.

'End of the lunchtime rush?' She cast a hopeful eye round the suddenly deserted underwear department.

'Give it five minutes, then it'll be the afternoon surge of mothers and daughters.'

'Plain cotton for school,' agreed Lowri, tidying a rack of lacy silk teddies. 'I wish I hadn't taken early lunch— I'm starving already.'

'Then you'd better have tea with me later,' said a voice with a familiar, attractive lilt, and Lowri looked up in astonishment to meet a pair of blue eyes bright with accusation.

'Sarah!'

'In person. And I hope that blush is guilt, Lowri Morgan,' said her cousin, plainly incensed. 'What on earth are you doing here?'

'Working,' said Lowri lamely.

'I managed to puzzle that out for myself,' retorted Sarah. 'When did all this happen, may I ask? And why didn't you let me know?'

Lowri cast a hunted eye at some approaching customers. 'I meant to soon, cross my heart. Look, I can't talk now. I get a tea-break at three. Could you meet me upstairs at the coffee-shop?'

'You bet I could—ask for extra time.' Sarah fixed her young cousin with a steely eye. 'You've got some explaining to do, young lady. In the meantime I'll take one of these in thirty-four. And I'll come back to collect you at three. Be ready.'

Lowri found the required size quickly, wrapped the purchase and took her cousin's money, promising to see her later, then dealt with a pack of skinny, black-clad girls in leather jackets, all demanding the same make of maximum-bounce, minimum-price bra. For the next hour or so Lowri sold underwear of every category from sensible cotton sports to shameless see-through numbers of the type she'd never possessed herself nor ever dared to. It was some time before she got the chance to beg an extra ten minutes to add on to her tea-break. She hurried back to her post afterwards to attend to a tall man who was contemplating a display of astronomically pricey trifles with no hint of the dogged embarrassment most male customers displayed in the same circumstances.

'May I help?' said Lowri, in her usual friendly manner.

He smiled down at her, gold-flecked hazel eyes glinting under a pair of thick, ruler-straight eyebrows. 'I'm sure you can,' he said in a deep, drawling voice which flowed over Lowri like warm honey. He waved a hand at the exquisite lace bras. 'I want two of these things, and the other bits to go with them—one set in thirty-six C, the other in thirty-two E.' He cast an assessing eye over the display. 'The first lot in that pinkish colour, I think, and the other one black. Mmm, yes, definitely black.'

Lowri swiftly located the required sizes, riven with envy for the recipients. 'The knickers come in two styles, sir, the brief and this type.' She pointed out a sexy lace G-string.

He grinned lazily. 'The brief in pink, the non-existent one in black.' He raised one of his distinctive eyebrows. 'You approve?'

Lowri nodded, pink-cheeked. 'A popular choice, sir. Would you like them gift-wrapped?'

Her customer, as she'd expected, not only wanted them gift-wrapped, but clearly marked as to which was which, a male request familiar to her after four hectic weeks in the underwear department. And normally Lowri prided herself on deftness and speed at gift-wrapping, but under the bright, amused scrutiny her fingers changed to thumbs, a condition which worsened as Sarah bore down on them, tapping the watch on her wrist.

Lowri threw her an apologetic smile, but Sarah was staring at the man tucking his credit card back into his wallet.

'Adam!' she said in surprise. 'What are you doing here?'

The man grinned and kissed her on both cheeks. 'What do you think I'm doing, Sarah? I'm buying underwear.' He shot a look at Lowri. 'And damned expensive it is in this place.'

Sarah raised an eyebrow at the tempting packages. 'I bet I know exactly what you chose, too.'

'The same stuff Rupert buys you, I imagine,' he said, the grin wider, and looked at his watch. 'Let me ply you with tea and sinful cakes upstairs.'

'Not today, thanks, Adam. I'm just about to feed my young cousin, Lowri, here. Lowri, this is Adam Hawkridge.'

Adam Hawkridge turned the bright gold eyes on Lowri again and held her hand rather longer than necessary as he gave her a white, mega-watt smile. 'How do you do, Lowri—a pleasure dealing with you. Let's all have tea together.'

To Lowri's intense disappointment Sarah refused briskly, telling Adam this was a girls-only bun-fight and she'd take a raincheck for another time. Wistfully, Lowri murmured something polite as Adam took his leave, then raced after him with the packages he'd forgotten.

'Your parcels, Mr Hawkridge!'

He swung round, smiling. 'Thank you. Pity about tea,' he added in an undertone. 'Another day, perhaps?'

Lowri blushed again, said something incoherent and hurried back to Sarah.

'Wow!' she said breathlessly. 'What a gorgeous man.'

Sarah shook her head emphatically. 'Not for you, love. Gorgeous he may be, but he's a notorious heartbreaker.'

'I wasn't thinking of *marrying* him,' said Lowri tartly. 'I'll just get my bag.'

Once they were settled at a corner table in the coffee-shop Sarah fixed her cousin with a commanding blue eye.

'Now,' she ordered. 'Talk! When did all this come about? Have you quarrelled with your father? Why haven't you been in touch—where are you living?'

Lowri bit into a profiterole with enthusiasm. 'I came up here a month ago, but no quarrel with Dad, since you ask. I'm squashed in with four other girls in a flat in Shepherds Bush *pro tem*, and I intended making contact soon, Sarah, really I did, but I—I wanted to get my bearings first.'

'Which doesn't explain why someone with perfectly good secretarial skills is selling underwear to earn a crust, Lowri Morgan,' said her cousin severely. 'I thought you had a steady job in Newport.'

'So did I. But my boss took early retirement, and bingo, no place for little Lowri.'

'Surely you could have found something in the same line?'

'Not easy. Besides——' Lowri shrugged, smiling wryly. 'It gave me the ideal excuse to get away. Right away.'

Sarah poured tea, frowning. 'You said no quarrel, but *are* there problems at home?'

'Only for me. Dad's in seventh heaven.' Lowri sighed guiltily. 'I keep telling myself my father's only forty-seven and very attractive and perfectly entitled to a second wife only a few years older than me. And I adore Holly. Really I do. But sharing a house with two newlyweds who can't keep their hands off each other—particularly when one of them is your father—is pretty hard to take, Sarah. I got a nice little cheque from my old firm in Newport, Dad gave me a bit more, and one of the girls I worked with knew someone who needed another flatmate up here, so I left the land of my fathers and managed to get this job pretty quickly, thank goodness. It's only part time, but it's financing me while I do some serious job-hunting.'

Sarah eyed her narrowly. 'And are you enjoying life more?'

Lowri pulled a face. 'I didn't at first. I was even feeble enough to feel homesick for a while. But I'm settling down now.'

'How did my favourite uncle take to the move?'

'Torn between objections to the idea, and euphoria at the prospect of privacy and solitude with Holly.'

'Are you jealous?'

Lowri thought it over. 'Not of Holly,' she said slowly. 'Only of what they've got together, I think. And Mum's been dead a long time. Dad deserves his happiness. Only I just couldn't stand playing gooseberry.' She smiled cheerfully. 'Anyway, enough about me. Tell me about Dominic and Emily—and that scrumptious husband of yours.'

'Rupert's the same, only more so.' Sarah smiled wryly. 'Up to his ears in his latest book and prone to vile moods when the flow doesn't flow, as usual. My son seems to have some of his father's brains, but a far sunnier disposition, thankfully, while Emily sails through life happy in the belief that everyone loves her.'

'Which they do!'

'Up to now,' agreed Sarah. 'But she starts proper school in the autumn, so things may change.' She gave

Lowri a militant look. 'I shall expect you for the day on Sunday—no excuses.'

Lowri smiled happily and got to her feet. 'Try to keep me away! Sundays in London can drag a bit.'

'Then why on earth didn't you get in touch before?'

'I didn't want to cadge, Sarah.'

'You, Lowri Morgan, are an idiot. But I understand—no one better,' added Sarah, and kissed her. 'I was just the same when I first came to the big city. Right, I'm off. Come any time after breakfast on Sunday—or even before, if you like.'

Lowri shook her head, chuckling. 'I'll come in time for lunch—but thanks, Sal. I'll look forward to it.'

As she fought claustrophobia in the Underground on her way home, then battled for tenancy of the bathroom later that evening, Lowri's mood remained buoyant as she thought of Sunday with the Clares in St John's Wood. Her cousin Sarah, one of the three beautiful daughters of the Reverend Glyn Morgan in Lowri's native village of Cwmderwen, near Monmouth, was the wife of Rupert Clare, a novelist bankable enough to sell film rights to his books. Sunday would be fun. And she would enjoy it all the more because she hadn't given in and invited herself as she'd longed to do ever since her arrival in London.

The Clares' house in St John's Wood was a large, light-filled house with a sizeable walled garden at the back, and a converted coach house which housed the family cars on the ground floor and provided a self-contained flat on the floor above for Rupert's constant stream of secretaries, few of whom stayed for long. After a heart-warming welcome from Dominic and Emily, Lowri looked up to see Rupert loping down the curve of the graceful staircase, hands outstretched, Sarah close behind him.

'Who's a sly one then, little cousin?' he said, shaking his head, then gave her a hug and a smacking kiss. 'Escaped from the claws of the dragon, I hear!'

'If that's your way of saying I've left home, yes.' She grinned up at her cousin's charismatic husband. 'Hello, Rupert, nice to see you.'

'You wouldn't say that if you'd had to live with him this week,' said Sarah with feeling. 'Mrs Parks is not only the least efficient secretary Rupert's ever had but also the most timorous, which brings out the sadist in him. She's driving the great author mad. And I flatly refuse to take over from her—but you don't want to hear about that. Come into the conservatory. We'll picnic in there to enjoy the April sunshine.'

With Emily clinging to her hand, and Dominic telling her all about the new school he was going to shortly, Lowri basked in the glow of Clare hospitality as she leaned back in a comfortable wicker chair, sipping happily from a tall frosted glass decorated with mint and slices of fruit.

'Pimms for us, fruit juice for the small fry,' said Rupert, handing a beaker to his daughter. 'You, Dominic, are promoted to the dignity of a glass.'

'Gee thanks,' said his son with sarcasm. 'Couldn't I have just a sip of Pimms, Dad?'

'No fear,' said his mother, smiling to soften the blow. 'There's the doorbell. Off you go to answer it, please.'

'Mummy says you live in London now,' said Emily, beaming up at Lowri. 'Why aren't you living with us?'

'I've got a flat,' said Lowri hastily, and Rupert snorted.

'Fifth share of one, I hear.'

'One girl is moving out next week, thank goodness.' Lowri pulled a face. 'Which means my rent will rise, but at least I'll get a room with a wardrobe, and more chance of the bathroom.' Her eyes narrowed suddenly at the sound of voices in the hall. One of them was vaguely familiar. She threw a questioning look at her cousin.

'We've got two other guests today, love,' explained Sarah. 'After I met Adam Hawkridge in your shop the other afternoon he rang up and invited us out to something he calls brunch today. I told him we had company and asked him here instead, which meant including the current girlfriend, as usual.'

As Dominic showed the new guests into the conservatory Lowri got to her feet politely, wishing she'd worn something smarter than jeans and a striped cotton shirt as she shook hands with a leggy, narrow-hipped blonde encased in a ribbed white cashmere dress which drew all eyes to her startlingly prominent breasts. Adam Hawkridge, Lowri was relieved to see, wore jeans older than her own, plus a sweater over an open-necked shirt. He smiled at Lowri in gratifying recognition.

'Well, well—the little cousin!' He clasped her hand warmly. 'This is my friend, Fiona Childe.'

Lowri murmured something suitable, then watched, amused, as the girl gushed over the house to Sarah, cooed at the children briefly then turned the full battery of her charms on Rupert.

'Miss Thirty-two E, black lace,' murmured a deep voice in Lowri's ear, and she stiffened, swallowing a giggle.

'Not today,' she couldn't help whispering. 'It would show through.'

'Really?' Adam grinned down at her as he accepted a drink from Rupert. 'How very interesting.'

'What's interesting?' demanded Emily.

'You are,' said Adam promptly and sat down with Emily on his knee, stretching out a hand to Dominic at the same time. 'Right then, you two, tell me what you've been up to.'

This man is preposterously attractive, thought Lowri as she watched him charm the children. Taken feature by feature, his heavy eyebrows and wide, slightly crooked mouth had no pretensions to good looks, and his forceful nose had suffered a dent at some time, but somehow the sum of it all added up to something irresistible. And quite apart from his looks Adam Hawkridge possessed effortless charm all the more powerful for the hint of steel under it all. Rake he might be, but a potently attractive one in every way, thought Lowri as she listened to the inanities Fiona was burbling about her hairdresser.

'That's a frightfully clever cut—where do you have yours done?' she asked, eyeing Lowri's boyish crop with interest. 'Is the colour natural or do you have it tinted?'

'Sloe-black, crow-black Welsh hair like Sarah's,' Rupert informed her.

'There's a man in the hair salon where I work,' explained Lowri. 'He did it half-price for me.'

'You're a hairdresser?' exclaimed Fiona, flabbergasted.

'No, I sell underwear.'

'In the West End, not door to door,' added Rupert, poker-faced.

'How fascinating,' said Fiona blankly, losing all interest in Lowri on the spot.

Adam Hawkridge, however, more than made up for the deficit. During the meal he installed himself next to Lowri, asking her all kinds of questions about herself in between telling Dominic and Emily about his recent trip to Japan.

'How's your father?' asked Rupert later, refilling wineglasses.

'Retiring soon,' said Adam, sobering a little.

'Does that mean you'll be in charge of the company?' asked Sarah.

'Afraid so. All good things come to an end, so no more globe-trotting for yours truly. I'll be a desk-bound sober citizen at last.' He grinned challengingly. 'Did I hear someone say "about time"?'

Fiona tossed back her hair, pouting. 'Does that mean no more Ascot and Henley and so on?'

'Afraid so—to the first two, anyway.' The hazel eyes gleamed suggestively. 'I might be able to fit in a bit of so-on now and again, perhaps.'

Fiona gave a little scream of laughter. 'O-o-o-h, Adam!'

Sarah and Lowri sprang up simultaneously to clear away, avoiding each other's eyes. They refused offers of help from the men, who went out into the garden with the children to play cricket, while Fiona remained firmly where she was, reclining on a wicker chaise with a pile of magazines.

'What does he see in her?' said Sarah in disapproval as she loaded the dishwasher.

'Oh come on, Sal, two reasons hit you in the eye! She's the black lace thirty-two E I sold him that day. Adam told me.' Lowri grinned as she stored salad in a plastic container. 'Mind you he's got someone else on the go, too. He bought the same things in angel blush, thirty-six C.'

'Typical! Next week he'll probably be back for more of the same in two quite different sizes.'

'Why do men go unfailingly for sexy underwear, I wonder? Does Rupert?'

Sarah nodded. 'Pretty pointless, really.'

Lowri eyed her cousin curiously. 'Why?'

'Because the minute a man sees you decked out in that stuff he wants to take it off, of course!'

Lowri blushed to the roots of her hair.

Sarah eyed her narrowly. 'Ah! You've already discovered that for yourself.'

'Only once.'

'Not a happy experience?'

'No. My social life was pretty uncomplicated up to then, just enjoying dates with blokes I'd been to school with, and one or two men I'd met through my job. Then disaster struck. I got emotionally involved.'

'What happened?'

'Not a lot. The object of my affections forgot to mention he was married, the pig. It put me off men for a while. And since I've come up to London I haven't met anyone at all.' Lowri smiled ruefully. 'I hoped I would, to be honest. But so far the streets of London aren't exactly paved with eligible males eager to buy me romantic dinners.'

'Oh, dear, oh, dear, we'll have to do something about you,' said Sarah, the light of battle in her eye. 'I'll ask Rupert——'

'No, you won't,' interrupted Lowri promptly, 'I came up to London to manage my own life, remember. Let me have a go at it for a bit on my own, please, Sal.'

Sarah patted her cheek. 'Sorry—interfering again. Come on, let's drag Miss Thirty-two E into the garden for some cricket.'

But Fiona refused to budge, too careful of her hairdo to set foot outside the conservatory. Sarah and Lowri left her to her magazines and went to join in some energetic fielding while the menfolk batted, bowled and kept wicket in turn.

'How about you, Lowri?' asked Adam, offering the bat to her. 'Fancy your chances?'

'I don't mind having a try,' she said demurely, and let him show her how to grip the handle correctly. She winked at Dominic, who grinned from ear to ear as Adam jogged down the lawn ready to deliver a nice, easy ball to the beginner. Rupert, hunkered down behind her to keep wicket, smothered a laugh as Lowri danced down the wicket to the tame delivery, smashing it away into the shrubbery with a perfect forward drive.

Adam stared, open-mouthed as Dominic raced to retrieve it. 'I see, I see,' he said ominously, scowling at Lowri. 'Having me on, were you?' He put up a hand to catch the ball then came sprinting down the wicket in earnest, letting fly a full toss which Lowri swiped over his head with ease to wild applause from the four Clares. She dealt with his three successive deliveries with equal disrespect, until she grew careless and lofted a ball which Dominic sprang up and took spectacularly with one hand, winning concerted applause all round, loudest of all from the bowler.

Adam came sprinting towards Lowri, his eyes hot with accusation. 'Don't tell me that was beginner's luck!'

'Nah!' said Dominic scornfully. 'Her Dad's captain of the village cricket team where Lowri comes from. He taught her to play cricket when she was littler than Emily.'

'No son, you see,' said Lowri apologetically. 'Dad had to teach his skills to me. Not,' she added, 'that I get to use them much.'

Adam grinned. 'Did he teach you to bowl, too?'

'Only tame medium pace stuff.'

He handed her the ball. 'Right. Come on, then.'

'It's my turn to bat,' pointed out Rupert, aggrieved, as Adam took his stance in front of the wicket.

'Later—I want my revenge first!'

But Adam, swiping mightily at the third ball Lowri delivered, sent it straight through the window in the coach house office in a hail of broken glass, bringing the match to an early close.

Astonished by the howls of laughter from her hosts, Fiona burst from the conservatory to hurl recriminations at Adam, winning her deep disapproval from Emily, who slid a small comforting hand into his large one in consolation as he apologised profusely.

'Don't worry—Mrs Parks can type in the conservatory tomorrow,' said Rupert, clapping him on the shoulder.

With promises to settle the bill for the damage, Adam took reluctant leave, prompted by a petulant reminder from Fiona that they were expected for dinner elsewhere that night. Despite her urgings he took his time in parting from Dominic and Emily, even contriving a private word with Lowri while Fiona went upstairs to make unnecessary repairs to her face.

'For a pint-sized lady,' he said, his eyes glinting, 'you pack an almighty wallop, Lowri Morgan.'

'It comes in useful from time to time,' she admitted demurely.

'For beating off importunate lovers?'

'Not too many of those around,' she said candidly.

Adam Hawkridge shook his shiny brown hair back, frowning. 'Why not?'

'I wish I knew,' she said without thinking, then regretted it as she saw the gleam in his eyes.

'It's not personal preference, then? You don't have anything deep-seated against my sex?'

'Not too deep-seated, no,' she said warily.

'Splendid.' He smiled and shook her hand. 'I'm very glad Sarah invited me here today. Goodbye, little cousin.'

Lowri, pressed to stay for supper once the others had left, accepted with alacrity. She helped Emily get ready for bed, read her a story, then gave Sarah a hand with the meal, which Dominic was allowed to share before he too went off to bed and left the other three alone. Lowri found herself listening with shameless avidity when Sarah and Rupert discussed Adam Hawkridge's future destiny as they lingered over coffee round the kitchen table.

'A bit of a playboy, our Adam,' mused Rupert, 'but a brilliant electronics engineer just the same, with a definite flair for marketing. He'll fill his father's shoes very ably—far more than his brother would have done.'

'Rupert was in school with Peter Hawkridge,' explained Sarah.

'I often spent part of the holidays with his family,' added Rupert. 'Adam was only a kid in those days, of course. Can't be much more than early thirties even now. He's packed such a lot in his life that one tends to forget his youth.'

'Why isn't his brother taking over the business?' asked Lowri.

'He's dead, pet. Smashed himself up in his car when his wife went off with another man. Adam was at Harvard Business School at the time.'

'Gosh, how tragic. What sort of business is it?' added Lowri, trying not to sound too interested.

'Hawke Electronics rents software to a worldwide clientele. Adam's father built the company from scratch, and believes in ploughing back a fair percentage on research and development.' Rupert held out his cup for more coffee. 'And since Adam's return from the States the number of software programmes they provide has tripled. He's one bright cookie, our Adam. Dan Hawkridge is damn lucky to have such an able son to follow in his footsteps.'

'Adam switched off a bit at the prospect at lunch, though, wouldn't you say?' said Sarah, joining her husband on the sofa.

Rupert put his arm round her. 'The weight of future responsibility, I suppose. Once Adam's in charge, Dan's taking his wife off on the world cruise he's promised her.'

'In the meantime Adam will work his way through as many Fiona types as possible, I suppose, before he knuckles down,' said Sarah acidly.

'Does his taste always run to brainless blondes?' asked Lowri, chuckling.

'I don't think our Adam specifies hair colour, precisely. His women do tend to be leggy and well endowed in the bosom department, now I come to think of it. Why?' added Sarah in alarm. 'You're not thinking——?'

'No, of course not,' said Lowri promptly. 'I'm neither leggy nor blonde, remember. I like Adam, that's all. Dominic and Emily like him, too.'

'They dote on him,' agreed their mother. 'Adam will make a good father when he's ready. Retired rakes always do.' She smiled up at Rupert. 'As I know from experience!'

CHAPTER TWO

LOWRI had very little time for daydreams about Adam Hawkridge next day. The department was short-staffed due to influenza, and she was run off her feet during working hours. When she got back to the flat, weary and footsore, she forced herself to do a thorough cleaning job on the room vacated that day by the outgoing occupant, spent the evening arranging her things, then took a much needed shower before allowing herself the luxury of something to eat.

As Lowri emerged from the bathroom, Barbara, the owner of the flat, told her she was wanted on the phone. 'Man. Very attractive voice.'

Lowrie flew to the telephone, blushing unseen at her own disappointment when she heard her father's resonant tones. She assured him she was fine, told him about her day with Sarah, promised to ring more often and sent her love to Holly, at which Geraint Morgan coughed, hummed and hawed and finally blurted out the reason for his telephone call. Holly was pregnant. Lowri would soon have a little brother or sister.

Lowri congratulated her father enthusiastically, assured him she was overjoyed, then put the receiver down feeling rather odd. Deciding it was lack of food, she made herself scrambled eggs in the poky, chaotic kitchen, added a pot of tea and took her tray back to her room, in no mood now to join the others in the communal sitting-room. Later she rang Sarah to share the news.

'You sound shattered,' said Sarah bluntly.

'I am, a bit. I'm really very happy for Dad, but it was a bit of a body-blow, just the same.'

'Only natural. You two were so close after your mother died. Not your usual father/daughter arrangement.'

'Sorry to moan at you, but I had to talk to someone.'

'I'm glad you did—I can moan at you in exchange. Rupert's Mrs Parks threw a wobbly today.'

'Why?'

'It started with the broken window in the office and the move into the conservatory while it was mended. Then Rupert topped it off with twice as much work as usual this morning because he was struck with inspiration last night and dictated into his machine into the small hours——'

'Sarah, can't you think of a way to keep him in bed?' gurgled Lowri. 'I'll get you a sexy nightie at cost, if you like.'

'Don't be rude!' Sarah retorted, then sighed heavily. 'Anyway, Mrs Parks has taken herself off, vowing never to darken our door again, and I'm saddled with the typing, heaven help me. I don't know how I ever coped with working for Rupert in the old days before we got married—too besotted with him to mind all the fireworks, I suppose.'

'Can I help? I get Friday and Saturday off this week. I could lend a hand then, if you like.'

'Oh, Lowri, *would* you? Rupert pays well——'

'I don't need money!'

'Of course you need money. Don't be a goose. Anyway we'll sort that out when you come.'

In the end Sarah insisted Lowri come for a meal on the Thursday evening and stay the night, fresh for work in the morning. Lowri needed little persuasion. A couple of days' typing for Rupert was a small price to pay for a stay in the airy, comfortable house in St John's Wood.

The coach house window was intact, and the comfortable little office behind it in perfect order when Lowri settled down to start work on Rupert Clare's current novel a few days later.

'First of all,' advised Rupert, 'read through the draft so far. Sarah's printed the disks Mrs Parks typed, so spend this morning familiarising yourself with the characters and the plot. There's a kettle and coffee and so on in the other room when you take a break, but come over to the house for lunch before you start on any typing.'

Lowri, long one of his most ardent fans, smiled happily. 'Right, boss. I'm looking forward to a sneak preview of the latest Rupert Clare bestseller—nice work if you can get it!'

'It may not be a bestseller,' he said gloomily. 'I'm tackling a new period for me in this one: dark deeds in fog-bound Victorian London.'

Lowri breathed in a sigh of pleasure. 'Sounds great to me.' She rustled the sheaf of papers on the desk. 'Right then, eyes down and looking for the next hour or so.'

The story gripped her so completely from the first paragraph that Lowri hardly noticed Rupert leave, and looked up at Sarah blankly when her cousin appeared a couple of hours later to announce that lunch was ready.

'Lunch?'

'Yes, you know—soup, sandwiches, stuff like that,' said Sarah, laughing, then frowned. 'No cups? Didn't Rupert tell you to make yourself some coffee?'

Lowri bit her lip guiltily. 'He did, but I forgot. I was so absorbed I didn't notice the time.'

'That's a novelty! Mrs Parks could never work for more than half an hour at a time without a dose of caffeine to keep her going.'

Lowri stood up, stretching. 'Sounds as though the lady's no loss.'

'She will be to me if I have to stand in for her,' said Sarah with emphasis. 'Come on. Dominic's in school, Emily's gone off to spend the afternoon with her chum, and Rupert's having lunch with his agent so it's just the two of us.'

It was pleasant to gossip with Sarah over the meal but Lowri was adamant about returning to the office after half an hour, eager to finish the first portion of the draft so she could start on the real work of typing up Rupert's next tapes. The novel, which bore all the hallmarks of Rupert's style in the vivid characterisation and complex, convoluted plot, was an atmospheric story of revenge.

'It's riveting,' said Lowri, as she finished her coffee. 'All that underworld vice simmering away behind a façade of rigid Victorian respectability. I can't wait to find out Jonah Haldane's secret!'

Lowri's enthusiasm resulted in more progress in one afternoon than the less industrious Mrs Parks had achieved in the two previous working days. When Rupert came to blow the whistle at six that evening he was deeply impressed, and obviously found Lowri's reluctance to call a halt deeply gratifying.

'Enough's enough for one day, nevertheless, little cousin,' he said firmly. 'Sarah says you're to pack it in, have a bath, then if you can bear it, read a story to Emily. We had to promise her that to keep her from storming your citadel hours ago.'

'Of course I will,' said Lowri, stretching. 'Though something a bit different from yours, Rupert.' She shivered pleasurably. 'It's a bit terrifying in places.'

'Sarah says you like it.'

'Like it! I can't wait to see what happens next.'

'You're very good for my ego, Lowri,' said Rupert as he walked with her across the garden. 'A little sincere encouragement does wonders. Writers get bloody depressed some days.'

'You needn't,' returned Lowri with certainty. 'This is your best ever, Rupert. And I should know. I've read every book you've written.'

He gave her a friendly hug and pushed her into the kitchen, where Emily and Dominic were eating supper while Sarah clattered saucepans on hobs set into an island which gave her a view of the large kitchen while she worked. At the triple welcome showered on her Lowri felt suddenly enveloped in something missing in her life since her father had married again: a sense of belonging.

'About time you knocked off,' said Sarah, waving a wooden spoon. 'The idea was to help Rupert out a bit, not work yourself to death, Lowri Morgan.'

When Lowri was packed and ready to return to Shepherds Bush, Rupert fixed Lowri with a commanding green eye.

'Sarah and I have a suggestion to make. Feel free to refuse if you want, but hear me out.'

Lowri looked from one to the other, her dark eyes questioning. 'I'm all ears.'

'It's about the work you've been doing for me——'

'Something wrong?'

'Wrong!' snorted Sarah. 'The exact opposite, Lowri. I'm the only one who's ever worked so well with Rupert. Though you haven't seen him in a tantrum yet,' she warned.

'Tantrum?' said Rupert, incensed. 'I may be subject to the odd mood——'

'Your moods are not odd, they're horrible,' corrected his wife flatly. 'Anyway, Lowri, the gist of all this is that if you're not totally dedicated to selling knickers Rupert wondered if you'd fancy working for him full time.'

Lowri's eyes lit up like stars. 'You mean it?'

'You bet your sweet life I do,' said Rupert emphatically. 'And what's more, you can pack in that flat and come and live here with us.'

'But I couldn't impose on you like that,' said Lowri swiftly.

'Not even in the coach house flat?' said Sarah, smiling. 'You can be as private as you like over there, live entirely your own life as much as you want, or be part of ours whenever the fancy takes you. We'd even take a small rent for the flat if it would make you feel any better.'

'Are you doing this because you feel sorry for me?' asked Lowri suspiciously.

'Don't talk rubbish!' Rupert patted her shoulder. 'It's you who'd be taking pity on me. I'm offering you the job, Lowri, because you do it so well. Better than anyone since the reign of my lady wife here. *And* you won't have hysterics if—when—I shout at you. Because shout I will when things go wrong, believe me. So before you answer you'd better think that bit over. But if you can stand my moods, and you fancy the job, how about it?'

From the day she moved her possessions into the Clares' coach house life was transformed for Lowri. The bed-sitting-room adjoining her little office was a comfortable little apartment, complete with bathroom and a minuscule kitchen just large enough for Lowri to cook a meal for one occasionally. After the flat in Shepherds Bush the privacy was wonderful, unmarred by the slightest tinge of loneliness, since at any time Lowri knew she could stroll down the long, beautiful garden to a warm welcome in the house. This, however, was a privilege Lowri rationed herself strictly from the start.

But there were definite advantages for the Clares in the situation, nevertheless, since Lowri was happy to act as baby-sitter when the busy social life of the Clares demanded it. Since the retirement of Mrs Dobson, Rupert's original treasure of a housekeeper, Sarah had taken on Brenda, who came in daily to help with the house. But Brenda enjoyed a hectic social life, and wasn't keen on baby-sitting too often in the evenings, which left a gap Lowri was only too glad to fill.

As the horse-chestnuts came into bloom and a green smell of spring came floating through her open office window, Lowri felt that fate had been very kind to her indeed. She sniffed at the heady vanilla scent of trees in blossom and heaved a contented sigh as she applied herself to the work which grew more absorbing by the day. The novel was now in its third quarter and working up suspensefully to the climax which Rupert flatly refused to reveal to Lowri in advance. Not even Sarah was any wiser, which apparently was nothing unusual. Rupert liked to keep his plot to himself until the very last sentence was recorded on tape.

Then one weekend Lowri's presence as a guest was commanded at one of Sarah's parties. And the tempo of life quickened again.

Lowri had helped out during the day, mainly by taking charge of Emily while Sarah concocted delicious cold dishes for the party meal, but once Dominic and Emily had eaten supper and the latter was settled in bed with a story Lowri dashed back to her flat to get ready, tingling with anticipation. She had a new, flattering black dress to wear, bought with her first cheque from Rupert, but, most important of all, Adam Hawkridge would be one of the guests.

The party, as always at the Clare home, was a lively, entertaining occasion from the start, and Lowri, circulating with platters of canapés, no longer felt shy as she mingled because so many of the guests were already well known to her by this time. Sarah, stunning in a plain white dress with turquoise and diamond hoops in her ears, her black hair coiled high on her head, was in her element at Rupert's side as they welcomed their guests, most of whom had some literary connection. But the guest who had none was nowhere in sight. Adam Hawkridge was late. Lowri found it hard to stop watching the door, but when he finally put in an appearance her heart sank at the sight of his tall, blonde companion. When he noticed Lowri his face lit with the familiar, blazing smile, and he threaded his across the crowded room towards her, leaving the voluptuous blonde with Rupert and Sarah, and another man new to Lowri.

'Hello, Lowri!' He squeezed her hand and took the silver dish from her, dumping it unceremoniously on the nearest table. 'How's the little cousin? Are you enjoying the new job? Is Rupert a despot to work for?'

'Hello—Adam,' responded Lowri shyly. 'I'm fine, the work is fascinating, and so far Rupert's very kind.'

'And so he should be.' He kept hold of her hand to take her across the room. 'Come and meet Caroline.'

'Where's Fiona?'

'Haven't the foggiest,' he returned carelessly. 'Out partying with some other guy, at a guess.'

When they joined the others Adam barely had time to make introductions before the man with Caroline moved in on Lowri with practiced expertise.

'I'm Guy Seton, Caroline's brother,' he announced, and took Lowri by the hand. 'Afraid I'm a gate-crasher. The delightful Mrs Clare assures me she doesn't mind.'

Lowri gazed into a pair of narrow, hot dark eyes under hair almost as fair as the sexy Caroline's, and felt an odd pang of apprehension. Guy Seton exuded such restless energy that he made her feel uneasy.

Rupert, who obviously did object to the gatecrasher, smiled warmly at Lowri. 'So there you are, little cousin,' he said, with emphasis on the relationship. 'Having a good time?'

'Too busy handing round food for that,' said Sarah, and flapped a hand at Lowri. 'Leave all that now. Brenda will help with supper.'

To her annoyance Lowri found herself neatly separated from the rest by Guy Seton. Adam, who had momentarily deserted Caroline for a delighted redhead on the far side of the room, spared a disapproving frown for Guy's manoeuvre, Lowri noted wistfully, as the latter hurried her through the open French windows on to the terrace outside. The slim, restless man perched on the stone balustrade, one leg swinging as he patted the place beside him.

'Come. Tell me your life story, little Welsh cousin. Was your father a fan of matchstick men—is that how you got your name?'

Lowri perched uneasily beside him, not at all happy about finding a constricting arm round her waist. 'No. Mine's spelt with a final "i" —Welsh for Laura, nothing to do with Lowry the artist. And my life-story isn't interesting in the slightest.'

'You interest me a bloody sight more than the so-called literati in there.' His arm tightened. 'What's a nice little Welsh maiden like you doing in the big city, Lowri with an "i"?'

She sat rigid in his clasp, disliking the innuendo he managed to inject into the word 'maiden'. 'I work for Rupert.'

'Lucky Rupert.'

Lowri shifted uncomfortably, but Guy Seton held her fast. 'Don't be frightened, poppet,' he said, chuckling. 'I shan't eat you.'

'Which reminds me—there's a perfectly good supper waiting inside,' she said firmly, and disengaged herself. 'Shall we go and sample some of it?'

Guy Seton possessed a thick skin, she found, quite impervious to her unsubtle hints that his monopoly of her company wasn't welcome. He stuck to her side like glue, and short of causing a scene there was nothing she could do about it. Something about his hectic, almost feverish attentions filled her with unease. Lowri had no illusions about her looks. She was more rounded than she would have liked for her lack of inches, and regarded her large, dark eyes as her only redeeming feature. Besides, she had good reason to distrust a sudden rush of attention like Guy Seton's, wary of men who came at the gallop after only one glance. And by staying so close all the time Guy was destroying her hopes of a chat with Adam at some stage. Not, she noted, depressed, that there was much chance of that. Adam had now returned his attentions to the sultry Caroline, who was smouldering up at him in a way which made it obvious she wanted him to round off the evening in her bed.

'Are you a friend of Adam's?' she asked Guy, her eyes on the absorbed couple across the room.

'Not a friend, precisely,' said Guy. His mouth thinned as he followed her gaze. 'I was in school with him. He's Caroline's "friend". She's crazy about him. Women flock round Hawkridge in droves. Can't think why. He's no oil painting.'

'No,' agreed Lowri. 'He's not.' But he's twice as attractive as you, Guy Seton, she added silently, because he's got warmth. You're a cold fish, I think, for all the burning glances and febrile charm.

'Caro's so blatantly panting to share Hawkridge's bed I'm amazed she insisted I came with them tonight. But I'm glad I did.' Guy gave her a smile of confident intimacy. 'Instead of playing gooseberry to those two, I can take you home instead.'

Lowri's answering smile was frosty. 'No need. I live here.'

'Hell.' He scowled. 'That's a blow.' He eyed her up and down, his eyes undressing her. 'Rupert Clare's bloody lucky, having two gorgeous women at his disposal under the same roof.'

Enough was enough. Lowri glared at him. 'I'm very fond of Rupert, but I live in the coach house to be precise, not under his roof. Nor am I at *anyone's* disposal.' She thrust her empty glass in his hand. 'Goodnight, Mr Seton.' And without another word she hurried through the hall to the kitchen and slammed the door shut behind her.

'What's up?' Brenda looked up from loading the dishwasher in surprise. 'Someone ruffle your feathers out there?'

'Someone certainly did,' said Lowri, seething. 'Any coffee going, Brenda? I'll give you a hand to clear away.'

'Coming up, love,' said Brenda, filling the kettle. 'Won't say no to a bit of help. Terry's coming for me in half an hour—mustn't keep him waiting.'

'Terry?' said Lowri, laughing. 'What happened to Wayne?'

Brenda winked, thrusting a hand through her spiky blonde hair. 'What he doesn't know about he won't grieve over, eh?'

A few minutes later Lowri stole along the pergola lining the path which led to the coach house. She gained her little sanctum with a sigh, partly of relief for eluding the disturbing Mr Seton, but mostly of regret for having so little opportunity to talk to Adam. Which was stupid, she told herself as she hung up the black dress. Any time he'd had to spare from Caroline had been spent on the redhead with the cleavage. She cleaned off her make-up irritably, rubbed some moisturiser into her olive skin, gave her lengthening hair a good brush and got into a nightshirt and the vividly embroidered black silk kimona her father and Holly had given her for Christmas, by which time she felt ominously wide awake. She slid into bed and reached for a well-thumbed copy of *Northanger Abbey*. Jane Austen's dry wit rarely failed to soothe, and with a sigh Lowri banked up her pillows, settled herself comfortably and put thoughts of Adam and the annoying Mr Seton firmly from her as she settled down to read.

She was halfway through the first chapter when a knock on the outer door brought Lowri bolt upright. She sprang off the bed, startled, and went out through the office, certain it must be Sarah or Rupert with some emergency. She unlocked the door then screeched in fright as Guy Seton pushed her back inside the office, slammed the door shut and stood with his back to it, a wild look about him which scared her rigid.

'Now, now, Lowri,' he said menacingly. 'This isn't at all friendly, is it? I need some comfort, some tender loving care, sweetheart.'

'Well, you won't get it from me!' she snapped. 'You shouldn't be here.'

'Why not? I asked if I could see you home. And here you are, and so am I. Let's party!' He stalked towards her, the restless, feverish aura about him now so pronounced that Lowri could have kicked herself for not recognising the cause sooner. Her unwanted visitor was obviously high on something a lot more dangerous than champagne.

'Guy, please,' she said, backing away. She tried to smile. 'It's late and I'm tired——'

'Then come to bed,' he said hoarsely, and reached for her.

Lowri fought him off savagely, but despite his slim build Guy Seton was strong; deceptively so. He managed to drag her, kicking and struggling, into the bedroom and on to her bed. Beside herself with rage, Lowri twisted and turned like an eel, her nails raking down his face, her teeth sinking into the mouth crushing hers, and Guy let out a howl and drew back, face contorted, clenched fist raised. Then suddenly he was flat out on the floor, felled by a savage blow from Adam Hawkridge, who stepped over the unconscious man without a second look, and hauled Lowri into his arms.

'Are you all right? Did that bastard hurt you?' he barked.

Her teeth were chattering so much Lowri found it hard to reassure him that apart from the odd bruise and the fright of her life she was fine.

'How—how did you know——?' she gasped.

'Caroline was ready to go home and insisted her blasted brother go with us. When I couldn't find him I made an educated guess. Thank the lord I did,' he added harshly, and tipped her face up to his. 'Were you saying the truth? He didn't—harm you?'

Lowri's face flamed. 'If you mean did he rape me, *no*! And I didn't lead him on, either—I swear I didn't.' Tears of reaction slid down her face. 'I just don't understand it. He stuck to me like glue all evening. In the end I got so fed up I escaped and came back here. But——' she gulped. 'He followed me. That's it, you know the rest.'

Adam held her close, patting her as though she were Emily. 'There, there, it's all over now. Shall I fetch Sarah?'

'No! And for heaven's sake don't say a word to Rupert, either.' She grimaced at the thought. 'His explosion threshold's a bit low, as you know. Let them finish the party in peace.' A convulsive shudder ran through her. She swallowed a sob and Adam's arms tightened.

He cursed under his breath and turned her face up to his. 'Don't, little one,' he said urgently, 'you're safe now.'

As her tear-wet eyes met his Lowri's heart gave a sudden thump and she breathed in sharply. For a moment they were utterly still, then Adam bent his head involuntarily to kiss her, the inflammatory effect of the contact so unexpected it took both of them by surprise. Lowri's lips parted to the sudden seeking of his tongue and Adam's arm tightened, his free hand cupping her head to hold her still as he kissed her with a fierce heat quite different from the comfort she knew was all he'd intended.

When he let her go, several earth-shattering moments later, Lowri almost staggered.

'Hell and damnation!' he said bitterly. 'I'm no better than Seton.'

Lowri blinked, dazed, trying to smile. 'Don't say that. You—you were just comforting me.'

Adam's eyebrows rose. 'Was I, Lowri?'

She flushed, and looked away, biting her lip in sudden disgust as she caught sight of Guy Seton, still out to the world on her bedroom floor. 'Ugh! What shall we do about—about that?'

For answer Adam bent down and slung the unconscious man over his shoulder with negligent ease. 'I'll just dump him in the back of the car and collect Caroline. I'll have to put her in the picture, I'm afraid, but no one else need know.' He manoeuvred Guy Seton's body through into the office, motioning Lowri to open the outer door. 'Is the coast clear?'

She peered around outside, nodded, then smiled up at him ruefully. 'I'm deeply grateful to you, Adam. I rather fancy you saved me from a fate worse than death.'

Adam gave her a sombre look. 'I feel responsible. I brought the bastard here tonight, after all. I'm very sorry, Lowri. For everything.' He paused a moment, a sudden, irrepressible gleam in his eyes. 'Well perhaps not *quite* everything,' he amended, grinning, and hefted his unconscious burden more securely, waved his free hand, then made his way down the outer stair and disappeared through the gate in the wall.

When he was out of sight Lowri locked her door and shot the bolts into place, then stripped her bed and put clean sheets on it, thrusting thoughts of Adam's kisses from her mind by concentrating fiercely on the debt she owed him. Without his timely appearance there could have been a great deal more to put right in her life than a mere change of bedlinen.

CHAPTER THREE

AFTER a restless night Lowri slept late next morning, and awoke at last to loud knocking on the office door. She jumped out of bed, pulling on her kimono.

'Coming!' she called, wincing at the pounding in her head, and went to the door to admit Dominic.

'Mum says will you come over? You've had a telephone call.' He eyed her in surprise. 'Gosh, Lowri, what a shiner! How did you get that?'

Since Lowri could barely see out of one eye, the question came as no surprise. 'I bumped into something,' she said with perfect truth. Guy Seton's elbow had rammed her eye while she was fighting him off. She smiled at Dominic. 'Tell Mum I'll be there as soon as I've dressed. I've been lazy this morning.'

One look in the bathroom mirror told her that trying to keep last night's events from Sarah would be a complete waste of time. The truth, Lowri thought, resigned, will out whether I want it to or not. She frowned, realising she'd forgotten to ask Dominic who'd rung her.

Later, dressed in jeans and an old checked shirt, Lowri put on dark glasses to shield her eye from the bright sunshine and crossed the garden to join Sarah and Rupert in the kitchen.

'Good morning,' she said, smiling brightly. 'Where's Emily?'

'Dominic's keeping her amused until you've told us about the black eye,' said Sarah promptly, pouring coffee.

34

Rupert plucked the glasses from Lowri and whistled. 'Hell's bells!' his eyes narrowed dangerously. 'Right. Tell me who did that, Lowri—now!'

'First tell me who rang,' she said quickly to divert him.

'It was Adam,' said Sarah, 'He's coming round later to take you out to lunch.' She eyed Lowri militantly. 'But never mind that—how on earth did you get that shiner?'

Lowri, trying to appear unaffected by the news that Adam intended taking her out, drank some coffee and gave a terse account of the encounter with Guy Seton. 'So you don't have to do battle for me,' she told an incensed Rupert at the end of it. 'Adam knocked Guy Seton cold last night on the spot. The man probably looks—and feels—far worse than I do this morning.'

'I should bloody well hope he does,' said Rupert savagely.

'Is the eye the only damage?' demanded Sarah urgently.

'Yes. Adam arrived on the scene before Guy could have his wicked way with me.' Lowri held out her cup for more coffee. 'But it beats me why the wretched man should have been so intent on getting it. I'm not the type who drives men wild, now am I!'

'You obviously appealed to Seton.' Rupert scowled. 'He took one look and kept sniffing round you all night. I would have done something about it, but he's quite attractive, I suppose. You might have wanted it that way.'

'I told you she wouldn't,' said Sarah with scorn. 'Guy Seton's bad news where women are concerned.'

'Another heartbreaker, like Adam Hawkridge?' asked Lowri slyly.

'Adam would never be so crass as to assault anyone,' said Sarah indignantly. 'Guy was in school with Adam, I admit, but otherwise he's not in the same class.'

'Beats me what he was doing here at all.' Rupert's jaw set. 'I'll have a word with Adam, find out why the devil he brought the chap along in the first place.'

'Caroline's idea, probably—Adam seems fairly smitten in that direction from what I could see,' said Sarah, and pushed a toast-rack towards Lowri. 'Eat something.'

'I'm not hungry.'

'Possibly not, but if you drink any more black coffee on an empty stomach you'll rattle like a castanet.'

Lowri gave in, and felt a little better afterwards, though angry with a fate which gave her a black eye for her lunch date with Adam Hawkridge. Any other time she'd have been on Cloud Nine at the mere thought of it. Even if he was smitten with Caroline.

'Go and change your clothes, slap on some lipstick,' advised Sarah, reading her mind. 'You'll soon feel more enthusiastic.'

Duly attired in a newish pair of cream denims, long pink cable sweater and dark glasses Lowri both looked and felt a great deal better by the time Adam arrived. She opened the office door to his knock, her smile wobbling slightly at the sudden, vivid memory of his kisses the night before.

'Hello, Lowri,' he said, smiling, and took her hand. 'I've rather press-ganged you into this, I'm afraid, but I wanted time alone with you to explain the drama last night.'

'It's very kind of you to take the trouble,' she said sedately, and took her time in locking the door to the flat.

'I've had a swift word with Sarah and Rupert to put them in the picture.' He ran down the stairs in front of her then turned at the bottom to hold out a steadying hand. 'Not unnaturally, Rupert feels responsible for you. He came down on me like a ton of bricks about my part in the affair.'

'But I told him you came to my rescue,' Lowri assured him as they left the garden by the side door.

'Rupert pointed out that if I hadn't brought Guy Seton no rescue would have been necessary. And he's right.' Adam's wide mouth twisted in disgust, then he smiled at her. 'Let's say goodbye then make for the open spaces. I've brought a picnic.'

Lowri gave him a delighted smile. 'What a brilliant idea!'

Adam suggested Runnymede, and a quiet spot near the river for their picnic lunch.

'The "banks of the sweetest river in the world" according to John Evelyn,' he told her later. He spread a rug for her, then opened a picnic basket to serve her with smoked trout pâté, cold chicken savoury with rosemary and garlic, a small bowl of green salad and crusty fresh rolls to eat with fierce farmhouse cheese.

'How did you manage all this on a Sunday morning?' asked Lowri, impressed. 'I bet King John didn't do nearly as well the day he signed the Magna Carta here.'

Adam's eyes danced beneath the heavy, straight eyebrows. 'My mother saw to it. I told her I needed to feed a very charming young lady from Wales. When she'd expressed her surprised approval—my usual female company tends more to smart nightspots than riverside picnics—she gave me some of the goodies intended for my father's lunch. Don't worry,' he added, as she gave him a startled look. 'There was more than enough left over—for them and several others. My mother's catering is generous.'

'Please thank her warmly on my behalf, and tell her how much it was appreciated,' said Lowri, surprised to find her appetite alive and well after all. 'This is lovely. All of it,' she added.

Adam leaned forward and gently removed the sunglasses, his eyes hot with sudden anger as he examined her eye. 'Exactly how did that happen?' he asked harshly, giving her back the glasses. 'If the swine hit you I'll go back and break his jaw this time.'

Lowri hastily explained her accidental contact with Guy Seton's elbow. 'He was obviously high on something. Wouldn't take no. Heaven knows why—I never gave him the slightest encouragement,' she added irritably.

Adam looked grim. 'He didn't need any. The girl he lives with gave him the push yesterday. She delivered an ultimatum. He was to see sense about his cocaine habit or she was leaving. Seton objected. She could take him with all faults or not at all, since, I quote, he could pull any woman he wanted any time, and would prove it.' Adam's jaw tightened. 'He stormed round in a state to Caroline, who's always adored him. She was terrified to leave him on his own, and, knowing I'd refuse if she told me why, she insisted we take him with us to the party. You were the obvious choice for Seton to make good his boast. I'm sorry. I should never have let the bastard anywhere near you, Lowri.'

'It wasn't your fault,' she assured him, and smiled. 'Now let's forget about Guy and just enjoy the sunshine. We don't get enough to waste it, and tomorrow I'll be back at my desk. Not that I mind,' she added happily, 'I can't wait to find out what happens next in Rupert's novel. We're approaching the climax of the story.'

'He's a master of his craft, I agree.' Adam smiled. 'And damn lucky to find someone willing to work so hard for him.'

Lowri shook her head. 'The luck's all mine. When I left home I never dreamed I'd find something so interesting to do, especially with a flat thrown in. I owe such a lot to Sarah and Rupert.'

He eyed her curiously. 'Why were you in such a hurry to leave this home of yours?'

Lowri looked away. 'Dad and I have been closer than most, but now he's got Holly it's only fair to leave him to his new life without me in the way. Especially now Holly's pregnant.'

'Ah. Do you mind that?'

'No—at least not now. It was a bit of a shock at first. Though I should have expected it; pretty obvious really from the way——' She stopped, flushing.

'I take it your father's very much in love with his new wife,' said Adam quietly.

'Exactly. And she with him.' Lowri turned away to investigate an insulated jug. 'Mmm, wonderful—coffee. Want some?'

They fell silent as they drank the dark, fragrant brew provided by Mrs Hawkridge. After a while Adam leaned over and took her hand.

'Never mind, Lowri. One day you'll marry and have a baby of your own, and no more regrets about your new little stepbrother—or sister.'

She withdrew her hand swiftly. 'My regrets were very short-lived, Adam.'

'Sorry.' He lay flat on his back, hands linked behind his head. 'Nevertheless I meant what I said. You're exactly the type for marriage and babies, Lowri Morgan.'

'Because I'm not blonde and voluptuous and a frequenter of fashionable haunts—like Caroline Seton and Miss Thirty-two E?'

Adam opened a disapproving hazel eye. 'That's not what I said. Those two are just to play with. You're the sort men marry.'

Lowri grinned impudently. 'Whereas you blench at the mere thought of marriage, I suppose!'

'How right you are. I've got too much to do to get married. When Dad retires, Hawke Electronics will be wife, mistress and family rolled into one. I'll have no time left over for the normal kind. All my energies will be concentrated on the company.'

Such a waste, thought Lowri, her eyes on the powerful, sprawled figure.

'Besides,' said Adam, his eyes closed, 'I've good reason to be allergic to the sanctity of marriage.'

Lowri sat very still. 'I heard what happened to your brother, if that's what you mean.'

'I do. I keep thinking I could have prevented what happened if I'd been home. Stupid really. Peter was always a highly strung, sensitive sort of chap—nothing like me. But to end it all just because his wife walked out on him! Damned if I would—but enough of that.' Adam leapt suddenly to his feet, holding out his hand. 'Come on, let's pack this stuff back in the car and go for a walk.'

As Lowri strolled with Adam Hawkridge through the sunlit afternoon, it suddenly occurred to her that she was finally living out the fantasies she'd indulged in before coming to live in London. She was actually wandering over watermeadows with a tall, devastatingly attractive man, a thought which added such sparkle to her mood Adam showed gratifying signs of reluctance when he parted with her in Hamilton Terrace.

'I won't come in, Lowri,' he said, as he stopped the car. 'I should have been somewhere else half an hour ago, so give my best to Sarah and Rupert and tell them I took great care of their little cousin.'

'It was a lovely day. Thank you, Adam.'

He smiled at her and patted her hand affectionately. 'My pleasure too, Lowri. You're very sweet—take good care of yourself.'

Lowri hesitated, then gave him a funny little smile. 'Can I ask you a very personal question, Adam?'

He grinned. 'Feel free.'

'Is Caroline the thirty-six C angel blush?'

Adam threw back his head and roared with laughter, then squeezed her hand, winking at her. 'Actually, no. You haven't met Miss Thirty-Six.'

Lowri shook her head, laughing, waved him off then reported in to Rupert and Sarah. She took herself off to her own little domain later to reflect on the day and wish, rather irritably, that Adam thought of her as something more exciting than the Clares' nice little cousin. She'd hoped against hope that he'd kiss her again, so she could show him she was all woman as well as just 'sweet'. Sarah was right, she thought moodily, as she lay in a hot bath. Adam Hawkridge was a heartbreaker of the most dangerous type of all—totally unaware of his own power.

Lowri buckled down to work with a will next morning, determined to put Adam Hawkridge firmly from her mind. Rupert had almost finished dictating his novel. In a day or two he would have given her all the tapes and by the end of the week Lowri hoped to finish typing the first draft.

'Then you'll have to type the whole thing all over again, and not just once but several times, probably,' warned Sarah. 'Rupert's rarely satisfied with it until about the fourth or fifth draft. Do you think you'll cope?'

'Of course I will,' said Lowri cheerfully, then raised an eyebrow. 'What happens when it's finally finished? Does that mean I'm out of a job?'

'Of course not! Rupert's already got the next book in mind. You'll be needed to research for ages before he actually starts on it. Which, I warn you, means long hours shut up in libraries, or lugging home weighty tomes to search for some obscure detail Rupert can't do without.'

Lowri beamed, delighted. 'Sounds great to me. History was my best subject at school.'

Rupert finished dictating his novel by mid-week and Lowri finished typing it late on the Saturday evening, ignoring all protests from the Clares about working on a weekend.

'I just have to know how it ends,' she said firmly, and refused to budge from her desk until the last line was typed. She sat back with a sigh at last, her mind buzzing with Jonah Haldane and his triumphant victory over his adversaries.

'Well?' demanded Rupert, when she went over to the house later to say she'd finished. 'What do you think?'

Lowri heaved a great sigh. 'It's utterly magnificent, Rupert.'

'Not recycled Dickens, then,' said Sarah with satisfaction.

'Sarah! What a horrible thing to say.'

'Rupert's description, not mine. I haven't even read it yet.'

Lowri turned on Rupert in fury. 'Don't you dare say that, Rupert Clare! I've never dared admit it because I seemed to be in a minority of one, but Dickens always bored me rigid. Whereas your book——' She waved her hands, searching for the right word. 'I can't express myself like you, Rupert, but what I'm trying to say is that when I came to the last line I wished desperately that I hadn't finished it, that I was starting at the beginning again. And this is just the draft—think of the impact when you're finally satisfied with it!'

Rupert threw his arms round her, laughing. 'All right, you little spitfire. Every novelist should have a champion like you. How long will it take you to print the last bit?'

'By Tuesday, I should think—Monday if I work tomorrow.'

'Definitely not,' said Sarah firmly. 'Rupert's giving you a treat tomorrow. At least I hope it's a treat—Dominic's sure you'll be thrilled.'

'Would you like to watch some Sunday cricket at Lord's?' said Rupert. 'Sarah's taking Emily to some birthday party, so how about coming to see Middlesex play your beloved Glamorgan with Dominic and me?'

Lowri was just as thrilled as Dominic had predicted. Lord's cricket ground was within such easy walking distance of the house she'd been longing to get to a match there ever since moving to St Johns Wood.

'Dad will be green with envy,' she said with a sigh of pleasure.

Sarah smiled affectionately. 'Not every girl's idea of a fun day!'

'But then,' mocked Rupert, 'Lowri's a Morgan like you, by no means a run-of-the-mill type of female.'

After her week of gruelling work it was an enormous pleasure to Lowri to sit between Dominic and Rupert at the famous cricket ground, applauding with partisan enthusiasm as she watched the Glamorgan eleven pull out all the stops against Middlesex.

'This is my second picnic in the space of a week,' she commented happily as they shared the picnic she'd helped Sarah pack earlier. 'Only this time I've got cricket as well and I adore one day-games. Dad's such a purist that he looks down on Sunday cricket, but I think it's exciting. Thank you so much for bringing me, Rupert.'

'I want to be a professional cricketer,' said Dominic indistinctly, wolfing a pork pie. 'I hope I'll be picked for the first eleven when I get to Shrewsbury.'

'Of course you will,' said a familiar voice, and all three turned round to see Adam Hawkridge laughing down at them. 'Make a few more catches like the one you saw Lowri off with and you can't fail. Greetings, everyone. May I join you?'

Rupert sprang to his feet to welcome the newcomer, Dominic beaming as he made room for Adam between himself and Lowri.

'You were lucky to find us in this crowd,' said Rupert, offering him a sandwich.

'I rang Sarah—she told me roughly where you'd be.' Adam smiled down at a suddenly shy Lowri. 'I gather this is your reward for working so hard.'

'Not every girl's idea of a treat,' said Rupert indulgently.

'Actually I rang up to see if you were free tonight,' said Adam, accepting a second sandwich.

'Me?' enquired Rupert blandly.

'No, thanks, you're not my type!' Adam grinned, then turned to Lowri. 'It was this lady I was after. I realise it's short notice, but I wondered if you'd care for a meal tonight somewhere and a film afterwards?'

Lowri bolted an unchewed morsel of sandwich whole, eyes watering. There was nothing in the whole wide world she'd have liked better, but that was hardly the point. Caroline, or Fiona, or Miss Thirty-Six C or one of probably a dozen others must have let him down at the last minute, leaving him at a loose end. She smiled politely. 'How very kind. But I'm afraid I'm tied up tonight.'

Adam stared in surprise, the wind very obviously taken out of his sails. He pulled himself together, smiling rather stiffly. 'My bad luck. I suppose it was a bit optimistic to expect you to be free. Another time, maybe?'

Lowri returned the smile non-committally, then rummaged in the picnic basket, conscious of the narrowed look Rupert turned on her. 'Anyone for an apple?'

When they got back to the house Lowri listened to a spirited account of the birthday party from an excited Emily, volunteered to put her to bed and read a story, declined supper on the excuse of the large picnic tea, and took herself off to mope in her own quarters.

An hour or so later Sarah knocked on her door and asked if she could come in for a while.

'Of course.' Lowri, glad of relief from her own morose company, went to put the kettle on for coffee.

'You can tell me to go away, if you like.'

'Of course I don't mind.' When Lowri returned with a tray she eyed her cousin sheepishly. 'I suppose Rupert told you Adam asked me out tonight.'

'He did, indeed.' Sarah ran a hand through her long dark hair thoughtfully. 'His account of the afternoon was very interesting. Adam obviously expected you to consent with maidenly—but prompt—gratitude and, I am told, seemed a bit put out when you refused. And since I know perfectly well you had no plans for this evening, unless you count washing your hair, or a date with a good book, I'm agog to know why you turned Adam down.'

'I thought you'd have worked that one out for yourself.' Lowri smiled ruefully. 'He was so confident I'd say yes, you know! Besides, he's dangerous—he frightens me.'

'You're not worried he'd behave like that beastly Seton man!'

'Of course not. But you were the one who warned me, remember. The first time I laid eyes on Adam Hawkridge you told me he was a heartbreaker. You were right. I could like him a lot—far too much for safety. If I see too much of him I could get my fingers burnt a second time. So I refused. Besides,' added Lowri tartly, 'I objected to the way he breezed up at the cricket match, expecting me to accept with humble gratitude because somebody else stood him up tonight.'

'How do you know that?'

'What other reason could there be? I've got my pride, Sarah. It was pretty obvious he expected me to drop everything and run.' She sniffed. 'No chance.'

'Rupert was deeply impressed,' said Sarah, smiling. 'Adam's such a charmer that at a guess I'd say no woman's ever said no to him in his life before, unless it was his mother, who's absolutely lovely, by the way. A nice polite little no from you probably did him the world of good.'

'I hope it did—because it didn't do *me* any good at all,' sighed Lowri despondently. 'It quite spoiled my afternoon—and to cap it all Glamorgan lost by one measly run!'

CHAPTER FOUR

LOWRI soon learned she'd hit on the one tactic likely to secure her Adam Hawkridge's interest whether she wanted it or not. Next day she answered the newly installed telephone extension in her office with a chuckle.

'Rupert, you must be psychic—I was just going to ring you. These hieroglyphics of yours on page thirty——'

'Sorry—I'm not psychic and I'm not Rupert either,' said a deep, satin-smooth voice. 'Adam here, Lowri. Rupert put me through to you. How are you?'

Lowri blinked. 'Adam! What a surprise. I'm very well, also very busy. How are you?'

'Offended. I spent a very lonely evening last night after you turned me down.'

'How sad.'

There was a pause. 'Lowri,' said the caressing voice. 'Was your refusal some kind of dressage by any chance?'

'Dressage?'

'Playing hard to get,' he said indulgently.

'Oh, but I'm not. Playing at it, I mean.'

Another pause.

'I thought we got on rather well together,' he went on, the banter suddenly gone.

'If you mean we had a pleasant time by the river, of course we did.'

'Then have dinner with me. How about Saturday?'

'Sorry. My weekend's booked.'

She heard him breathe out slowly.

'I won't give up,' he warned. 'You'll say yes to me sooner or later, Lowri.'

Don't hold your breath, she thought. 'Thank you for ringing, Adam. Goodbye.'

Lowri put the phone down with an unsteady hand, her heart beating like a drum. The mere sound of Adam's voice was more than enough to throw her off balance, which only confirmed how sensible she was to refuse him. It just wouldn't do to get involved with Adam Hawkridge. Not, she thought wryly, that she required a man to declare himself eligible before she'd have dinner with him. Not normally, anyway. And with any other man in the world it wouldn't matter. There was no danger of falling in love with someone else because... Her teeth sank into her lower lip as she stared in sudden dismay at the computer screen. Because she was already in love with Adam Hawkridge? Rubbish! She'd only met the man a few times. Not that it made a blind bit of difference, it was true just the same. She ground her teeth impotently. What a bird-brained idiot, to fall for a man allergic to emotional commitment!

Lowri took in a deep breath and pulled herself together. Now she'd faced the truth she'd get over it eventually, which meant avoiding Adam like the plague. Without fuel a fire would go out. She'd make it go out. And this time there was no white lie involved. She *was* booked for the weekend. Rupert was giving a lecture at a literary seminar, and she'd volunteered to move into the house to stay with Emily and Dominic so that Sarah could go with him.

Once they'd waved their parents off, Emily and Dominic helped Lowri get supper, ate it happily with her at the kitchen table and helped clear away afterwards with such conscious virtue that Lowri couldn't help laughing.

'Don't try to be *too* good, you two, or you'll burst by the time your mother gets back on Sunday.'

'Daddy said I must be an angel,' said Emily with a worried frown.

'Some hopes,' said her brother scornfully. 'You've got to die before you can be an angel, silly.'

Emily stared at him in horror, her lower lip jutting ominously. 'I don't want to die,' she quavered. 'Not before Mummy gets home.'

'Absolutely no chance of that,' said Lowri briskly, 'not with me around. Now then, *cariad*, race you up to the bathroom—if you win you choose the story.'

Some time during the protracted process of getting Emily to bed Lowri heard the telephone ring a couple of times, but left Dominic to answer it. Later, after she'd allayed Emily's fears about growing wings, and settled the little girl to sleep, Lowri went down to find Dominic just coming in from the garden.

'Who was on the phone?' she asked him.

'Sorry—didn't hear it ring. I was out in the practice net Dad put up for me. I'll check the answering machine.' Dominic went off, whistling, while Lowri checked that all the doors were locked.

'Two for you,' he reported, coming back to the kitchen. 'One was your Dad and the other was Adam.' He eyed her pink cheeks with interest. 'Do you like Adam, Lowri?'

'Of course. He's very nice,' she said sedately.

'I think he fancies *you*! All right if I watch television now?'

Lowri nodded, rather touched that he was asking her permission. 'I'll join you in a minute.' She went into Rupert's study to listen to the messages. Her father's voice enquired if she were well, but Adam's message made her bristle by ordering her to ring back immediately.

Lowri had a chat with her father and Holly, but ignored Adam's orders. Pleased with her iron self-control, she went off to join Dominic in front of the television, and when Sarah rang later Lowri made no mention of Adam's call.

'I hope the weekend won't be too tiring for you, or too dull,' said Sarah.

'Of course it won't. Stop worrying and have fun!'

After breakfast next morning Lowri drove Emily to her ballet class, dropped Dominic off at a friend's house for the morning, then went back to make the chocolate cake she'd promised as a treat. As she was sliding the tins into the oven the phone rang.

'At last!' said the spine-tingling voice. 'I've found you, Lowri Morgan.'

'Who is this?' she answered calmly.

'Adam—as you well know. Why didn't you return my call last night?'

'By the time I heard the message it was late. I assumed you'd be out.'

'I'm not out every night,' he cut back. 'In fact I was working my socks off until very late. It occurs to me that you could have meant you were just booked up in the evenings this weekend, so how about lunch today— or tomorrow?'

'Sorry.' Lowri explained the situation. 'I really must dash, Adam, I've got a cake in the oven. Bye.'

'*Lowri*——!'

She put the phone down swiftly before her resolve weakened, and rushed back to the kitchen to make herself a cup of extra-strong coffee. As she drank it she tried hard to quiet a small voice which asked her why she was giving Adam such a hard time. You might be the very one, it said insinuatingly, to change his mind about commitment, even marriage. In a pig's eye, she told it scornfully. I'm nothing much to look at. My face wouldn't launch so much as a dinghy, let alone a thousand ships. And Adam likes his women glamorous and skinny—except around the chest, whereas my shape's more the other way round. And if he does ask again— not that he will—I've just got to keep saying no.

When Lowri got back to Hamilton Terrace after collecting Emily and Dominic there was much excitement when they found a familiar convertible parked outside.

'Great! That's Adam's car,' said Dominic as Lowri drove into the garage.

'Is Adam coming to lunch?' clamoured Emily, and raced after Dominic towards the man reclining on the garden seat under the rose arbour. 'Adam, Adam!' she squealed, and launched herself into the arms held at the ready to receive her.

'Good morning, Miss Clare.' He said laughing and swung her round in a circle, then aimed a playful punch at Dominic.

'Mum and Dad are away.' Dominic grinned at him impudently. 'Lowri's looking after us.'

'Aren't you the lucky ones!' said Adam, smiling smugly as Lowri reached them. 'Nice to see you, Lowri— at last. I was just passing so I thought I'd call in.'

'Hello, Adam.' Conscious of the children's eyes on her, she managed a cool smile. 'I don't suppose you've time to come in, I know how busy you are.'

'All the time in the world—it's my day off,' he assured her, eyes dancing irrepressibly.

Emily tugged him by the hand to follow Lowri into the house. 'Come and have lunch with us—*please*, Adam. Lowri's made a cake.'

'I know,' he said, then laughed as Dominic's eyebrows shot to his hair.

'How? She hadn't started it when she took us out this morning.'

'I confess I rang up,' said Adam, unabashed. 'When I heard she was baking a cake, nothing could keep me away.'

'You rang her up last night, too,' pointed out Dominic.

'No law against it,' said Adam cheerfully. 'Tell you what, I'll give you a few balls in that net out there while Emily, like a perfect little angel, helps Lowri put lunch.'

'Emily doesn't want to be an angel,' said Lowri with a warning look, and gave the child a cuddle. 'Which is a very good thing. We like her just the way she is.'

'Who wouldn't!' said Adam swiftly and swept Emily up in a hug. 'Never did care for angels myself anyway— all that twanging about on harps!' As he put the child down Adam gave Lowri a straight look.

'*May* I stay for lunch?' he asked.

'Of course you can,' said Dominic impatiently. 'Come *on*, Adam!'

'I was asking Lowri. She's in charge.'

She gave him a fulminating look, then shrugged. 'If you've a taste for pasta and chocolate cake, by all means join us.'

'That's settled, then,' said Dominic and gave Lowri a conspiratorial wink. 'Adam can clear away afterwards instead of me.'

Once Adam's company was inevitable Lowri decided she might as well relax and enjoy it. Both children very obviously adored him—it would be a shame, she assured herself, to spoil their pleasure in the unexpected visitor.

During the meal, which Adam praised with extravagance, there was a heated discussion on how to spend the afternoon now it was raining. Dominic wanted to go swimming, while Emily pleaded for the rare treat of a trip to the cinema. With all the skill of a career diplomat Adam settled the argument by the simple expedient of agreeing to both.

'We'll all go off to see *Beauty and the Beast* this afternoon, then you and I, Dom, will bring the ladies home and go for a swim on our own.' Adam smiled at Lowri challengingly. 'We'll fetch a takeaway back with us—give Lowri a break from catering.'

'You're staying to supper too?' Dominic let out a warhoop of delight.

With Emily cuddled on his lap Adam eyed Lowri warily as she loaded the dishwasher. '*Do* you object?'

'Since you've won the majority vote, how can I?' she said tartly, then smiled at Emily. 'Go and wash the chocolate smudges off your face, darling. You too, Dominic, please.'

Emily slid off Adam's knee obediently, then looked up at him with cajoling green eyes. 'Can I sit by you at the cinema, Adam?'

'You certainly can.' He ruffled her black curls. 'Only hurry up. Nearly time to go.' He smiled at Lowri as the child trotted off happily after Dominic. 'Imagine the havoc that young lady will wreak when she grows up. One look from those eyes of hers and she'll have every man in sight at her mercy.'

'A bit like you, really,' observed Lowri, putting the remains of the chocolate cake in a tin.

Adam glared. '*What*?'

'Your eyes aren't green exactly, but aren't most women at your mercy when you smoulder at them?'

'Rubbish!' His mouth twisted in distaste. 'Besides, if that's the case why am I so bloody unsuccessful where you're concerned?'

'You're just not my type.' She smiled at him sweetly. 'You're so much older than me, for a start.'

His eyes narrowed dangerously. 'I'm not quite over the hill yet, Lowri Morgan—on any count!' He sprang to his feet and stalked towards her, then stopped dead as Dominic came rushing into the room with a packed sports bag. The boy halted, looking from one to the other.

'Were you two quarrelling?'

'Certainly not,' said Lowri, and went off to fetch Emily.

At the cinema Lowri managed to arrange things so that Emily was between herself and Adam, with Dominic on his far side. But before the film began Emily asked to go to the cloakroom. When Lowri took her back to the others Adam quickly installed Emily between himself and Dominic, forcing Lowri to take the seat next to him.

Once the award-winning music began, Emily was entranced. Even Dominic, who'd been rather superior about indulging his sister with her choice of film, was soon engrossed, something which Lowri was thankful for when Adam's hand captured hers and retained it in a relentless grip impossible to loosen without making a scene.

No fan of cartoon films herself, Lowri found the afternoon very long, deeply conscious of the warm dry clasp which never slackened throughout the entire film. To her relief Adam released her hand before the lights went up, but not quickly enough to escape Dominic's astute green eyes, one of which drooped in a knowing wink as he grinned at Lowri.

Adam drove them back to Hamilton Terrace, deposited Lowri and a tired, excited Emily at the house, then whisked Dominic off for a swim at a surprise location.

While they were gone Lowri supervised Emily's bath and sat quietly with the child afterwards, reading to her on the sofa in the small sitting-room the family used in preference to the rather formal drawing-room kept for entertaining. Emily burrowed against Lowri's shoulder drowsily, and dozed off for a while, but woke up with a start when Dominic came rushing in, blazing with excitement.

'*Guess* where we went—Adam's place! It's in this block of flats by the river, and there's this fantastic pool in the basement—there was no one there, we had the place to ourselves. I did *ten* lengths!'

'Fantastic! In that case you must be hungry. Where *is* Adam?' inquired Lowri.

'We stopped for a takeaway. Fried chicken and chips and things—he's just coming.'

Adam appeared in the doorway. 'I've dumped it all on the kitchen table, Lowri, will you come and supervise?' He bent over Emily. 'Hello, poppet, want some chicken?'

Emily shook her head. 'No. Thank you,' she added belatedly.

'Aren't you hungry, my angel?'

Emily glared at him and burrowed against Lowri. '*Not* an angel,' she sobbed.

'No, of course not, sweetheart,' said Adam, wincing as he met Lowri's glare. 'Shall I go and switch on an oven or something to keep the stuff hot?'

Lowri managed to soothe the child's sobs, motioned Adam to sit down and transferred Emily to his lap. 'You cuddle Emily, Dominic and I'll see to supper. We'll have it in here, for a treat.'

Once Adam exerted all his considerable charm on Emily she was soon laughing with him, though too tired to eat much.

'I think I'll take this young lady up to bed,' Lowri said after a while. 'Dominic, there's ice-cream or cake if you want pudding, and some cheese if you'd prefer, Adam.'

Adam sprang to his feet, holding out his arms for Emily. 'I'll carry her upstairs for you.'

'Thank you.' Lowri hurried up the curving staircase to Emily's small, pretty bedroom, then took the drowsy child from Adam. 'I don't think we'll bother with a bath tonight.' To her surprise Adam insisted on staying to help her undress the little girl, holding Emily on his lap while Lowri sponged her face, then watching as the child was tucked up in bed.

'She looks like a little angel, lying there,' he whispered.

Lowri shook her head, laying a finger to her lips as she went out of the room ahead of him. 'Never mention the word "angel" again, for heaven's sake. Emily discovered one's obliged to die before getting to be one, something she objects to violently, particularly before Mummy gets home.'

'Oops!' Adam grinned ruefully. 'I don't know much about children. I obviously put my foot in it.'

'Your famous charm soon won her round,' Lowri assured him tartly. 'I'd better clear up the remains of our supper—which I haven't thanked you for, by the way.'

He gave her a gleaming, complacent look as they went to join Dominic. 'I told you I'd get you to dine with me, didn't I! Not that I envisaged such a bizarre way to gain my ends.'

'Quite a change for you.' She gave him a crooked little smile and went into the sitting-room, where Dominic was glued to the television among the greasy remains of their impromptu meal. He jumped up guiltily, but Adam waved him away.

'My turn to help Lowri, old son.' He smiled at Dominic's open relief as the boy returned eagerly to his television programme.

Their disposable feast took very little effort to clear away, and once Sarah's kitchen was restored to its usual immaculate condition Adam volunteered to make coffee while Lowri checked all was well with her young charges.

When she got back she found Adam had mugs of instant coffee ready, instead of brewing Sarah's best Blue Mountain beans as Lowri had intended. She drank gratefully, just the same, feeling suddenly bone-weary.

'Right.' Adam's bantering manner dropped away like a cloak, his eyes steely as they challenged hers. 'Now that I've gone to such lengths to secure your company, Lowri, tell me the truth. Why did you turn me down?'

She eyed him curiously. 'Do I take it no one ever has before?'

Adam thought about it, then shook his head. 'Not that I can remember,' he said candidly.

Lowri decided to tell him half the truth. 'If you must know, Adam, I couldn't for the life of me think why someone like you should be interested in a girl like me.'

'Why the devil not?' he demanded, amazed.

'Oh come on,' she said scornfully. 'I've only met two, I admit, but Sarah says all your girlfriends run true to type.'

'What type?'

'You know perfectly well what I mean! Clothes, background, gloss, totally unlike me in every possible way. I'm a small-town girl, unsophisticated, and years younger than the women you usually go for. So it seemed only sensible to keep my distance from a notorious heartbreaker like you.'

Adam stared at her in blank distaste. 'Heartbreaker! What the blazes are you talking about?'

Lowri sighed. 'That's just it. You don't even know you do it. You turn that smile on a female, and give her that look that makes her feel she's the only woman in the world, say sweet nothings in that sexy dark brown voice of yours, then when she's putty in your hands you stroll off in search of the next conquest. You should carry a government health warning, Adam Hawkridge.'

CHAPTER FIVE

COLOUR flared in Adam's face then receded, leaving him pale and dauntingly grim.

'You're wrong!' he said cuttingly. 'My health is something I take great care of. In every way. I may enjoy the company of women but I'm no health risk to any of them, including you.'

Lowri blushed to the roots of her hair, her eyes bright with dismay. 'I had no intention—I mean the health warning bit was a joke, a stab at flippancy. I was referring to the heart trouble you inflict, nothing else!'

'Were you really?' He smiled sardonically. 'About time you grew up, Lowri. Hearts don't break. And I've never misled a woman in my life. I admit I enjoy the company of your sex, make the most of any privileges I'm offered—and I do mean offered—but always on the strict understanding that the arrangement's temporary. No strings and eyes wide open are the rules of the game. Permanence is out for me. At least for a good few years yet.' His eyes narrowed. 'You know, Lowri, if you expect some kind of commitment from every man who wants your company, you're likely to get pretty lonely.'

'I'm not that stupid!'

Adam gazed at her thoughtfully, an assessing gleam in his eyes. 'If you were any other woman I'd suspect your tactics.'

Lowri stiffened. 'What do you mean?'

'Frankly I'd take it as a ploy to arouse my interest, maybe even a bid to change my point of view.'

'Dream on!' she said scornfully.

57

The amusement faded. 'Then what is it, Lowri? Why won't you spend time with me?'

She smiled pityingly. 'Is it so hard to believe that I might just not want to?'

'Yes,' he snapped. 'It is. You enjoyed the picnic the other day.'

'Of course I did.' Lowri got up and cleared away the coffee-mugs. 'But I didn't realise it committed me—if you'll pardon the word—to come running any time you were at a loose end.'

Comprehension dawned in Adam's eyes. 'Ah, I see. The truth at last. You were annoyed because I asked you at such short notice.'

'That's right,' said Lowri glibly, glad he'd accepted her explanation at its face value. 'Now I'm sure you have other things to do tonight. Thank you for the trip to the cinema, Adam.' She held out her hand with deliberate formality. 'Perhaps you'll pop in on Dominic as you go out. I'll say goodbye here.'

Adam looked at the hand, then took it to pull her into his arms, holding her cruelly tight as he kissed her open, protesting mouth. Lowri struggled instinctively at first, but soon found Adam was a very different protagonist from Guy Seton. Adam was taller, broader, fitter, and even more intent on getting his own way. But his greatest advantage was Lowri's realisation that the pleasure she was experiencing was so intense it seemed a shame not to savour it. She yielded, and Adam took full advantage of it, kissing her until they were both shaken and breathless.

When he raised his head Adam's eyes glittered in triumph.

'You see?' he demanded, panting.

'See what?' she said unsteadily, thrusting her hair back from her flushed face.

'You asked what I saw in a girl like you. If I'm honest, Lowri Morgan, I think it's a lot to do with sexual chemistry.'

The words damped Lowri down like a cold shower.

'You don't like that,' he said, eyeing her warily.

Lowri shrugged and said nothing.

A smile played at the corners of his mouth. 'You'd prefer I was enamoured with your mind?'

Lowri looked at him steadily. 'It doesn't really matter, Adam. Either way I've no intention of adding my name to your list of conquests.'

Adam's lips compressed. 'Always supposing I'd any intention of suggesting that,' he said with heat.

She nodded, unruffled. 'True. Goodnight then, Adam. It was very good of you to help entertain Dominic and Emily. They had a lovely day.'

'Up until a few minutes ago, so did I,' he said bitterly, and with a curt goodbye he turned on his heel to go in search of Dominic.

Lowri passed a restless night in the Clares' guest-room, spending a major part of it convincing herself she'd done the right thing. In the long run, she told herself stringently, she'd be glad she'd resisted temptation and made her position clear to Adam. If she gave in and spent whatever time with him he wanted it was obvious he'd take it for granted they'd become lovers—a prospect which sent a slow, cold shiver down Lowri's spine. But eventually, probably sooner than later, Adam would grow restless and take off to seek pastures new. As he always did.

When she heard no more from Adam for a while Lowri tried hard to convince herself she was happy about it. The fact that she wasn't went unnoticed, mainly because she was working harder than she'd ever done on draft after draft of Rupert's novel. He was proving just as hard a taskmaster as Sarah had warned, but his moods had no effect on Lowri. She was glad of the work, just as determined as the author to arrive at a final jewel of a novel, cut and polished to the standard Rupert Clare's readers had come to expect.

When Rupert finally professed himself satisfied enough to let his impatient editor see the manuscript Lowri heaved a great sigh of relief and went home to Cwmderwen for the weekend, as she'd promised she would once her contribution to the book was finished.

'You realise the manuscript may come back for revision?' Rupert warned as he drove her to Paddington. 'For one thing the damn thing's probably too long. Tom Harvey will want me to cut it.'

Lowri stared at him in dismay. 'Oh, *no*—you can't! It's perfect as it is.'

'Did I ever tell you I loved you, Lowri Morgan?' said Rupert, chuckling. 'Only don't let my wife know I said that.'

'Sarah wouldn't mind a bit.' Lowri gave Rupert a wry smile. 'She knows you've got no eyes for anyone else in the world.'

'True. But it took quite a bit of persuading to make her believe that at one time.'

Lowri eyed her cousin's handsome husband consideringly as he brought the car to a halt in the station approach. 'I can well believe it.'

Rupert gave her a wry green look. 'Even the wildest rake settles down in time, Lowri, given the chance.'

'Always assuming he has the slightest inclination to do so,' she retorted, well aware he was referring to Adam. She took her grip from him. 'Thanks for the lift. I'll see you on Tuesday.'

Lowri enjoyed her weekend of peace and quiet, with nothing more demanding on the programme than watching her father play cricket and helping Holly prepare meals. And to her own secret relief she found she could tease Holly about her approaching motherhood with no trace of qualms about the advent of a new little Morgan. It made for a happy holiday all round, particularly since Geraint Morgan was well aware of the fact and grateful to his daughter for her reaction.

'You look a lot better,' said Sarah, when Lowri returned to St Johns Wood. 'Hardly surprising. A spell away from Rupert is a necessity now and again.'

'Not for you!'

'That's different. If Rupert and I fight we can make up afterwards—and enjoy it. But anyone who works for him needs a break from the famous temperament now and again. Come and have some lunch before you unpack.'

Over the meal Lowri gave the news from Cwmderwen, frank about her relief at feeling happy about the new baby. 'But I didn't go to church,' she added diffidently. 'It's not the same without Uncle Glyn.'

Sarah's face shadowed. 'No. The sudden shock of having my mother die first soon did for my father, and now he's gone I don't suppose I'll ever set foot in the church there again.' She blinked, and smiled brightly. 'But to change the subject, and cheer us both up, would you groan if I enlisted your help on Saturday?'

'Party?'

'Just a dinner. Ten of us. One of which,' added Sarah firmly, 'is you. And before you trot out your usual excuses, you won't be an odd female, Tom Harvey's coming.'

'His divorce came through recently, didn't it?'

'That's right. It's your job to cheer him up.'

'Thanks a bunch!' Lowri pulled a face.

After a few days deep in the fourteenth century, researching the Peasants' Revolt, Lowri thoroughly enjoyed a Saturday morning spent in helping with preparations for the dinner that night. Brenda was going through the rest of the house like Sherman through Georgia, and Rupert had volunteered to take his children swimming, followed by lunch in the restaurant of their choice.

'Which means cheeseburgers and milkshakes and the devout hope that Emily won't be sick afterwards,' said Sarah, as she concocted a sauce to serve with the salmon they were to eat later. 'What are you wearing tonight?'

Lowri pulled a face as she looked up from scrubbing tiny new potatoes at the kitchen sink. 'The black dress I wore to the last Clare soirée I graced, I'm afraid.'

'No afraid about it.' Sarah grinned. 'Beside, Tom was missing that night, so he won't have seen it.'

'I don't suppose he'd notice if he had.' Lowri pulled a face. 'What do I talk about to cheer him up, for heaven's sake? He's tremendously witty and erudite, according to Rupert. I'm frightened before I've even met the man.'

'All you do is mention Rupert's book and you're up and running.'

'I hope you're right!'

Lowri's evening began with a series of surprises, the first of which was the pleasant discovery that she'd lost a pound or two. The black dress was far less struggle to get into. Then while she was doing her face Rupert knocked on the door of the flat and presented her with a package.

'A small token of appreciation for all your hard work, Lowri.'

Deeply touched, she opened a box containing a silver filigree brooch shaped like a butterfly, with coral insets in its wings. 'Rupert, this is so lovely! But you had no need——'

'A bribe to ensure future labours,' he assured her, kissing her cheek. 'Hurry up. Come and have a drink before the others arrive.'

When he'd gone Lowri added a few more touches to her face than she usually bothered with, then pinned the new brooch just below her collarbone, delighted to find it quite transformed her plain little dress.

The third—and biggest—surprise confronted her in Sarah's drawing room. When Lowri saw Adam Hawkridge chatting with Rupert near the open french windows she stopped dead in her tracks, heart thumping as she fought the urge to turn tail and run.

Rupert beckoned her over with an affectionate smile. 'There you are, Lowri. Come and say hello to our unexpected guest. May I say you look ravishing this evening, little cousin?'

'You can say it any evening,' she returned flippantly, and walked towards them hoping her turbulence wasn't showing behind the bright, social smile she gave Adam. 'Hello there. I didn't know you were coming tonight.'

Adam took her hand and held it for a moment, his answering smile accompanied by the familiar gleam in his eyes. 'Hello, Lowri. Rupert's right. You look wonderful. And I'm afraid I'm a sort of gatecrasher—again.'

'Nothing of the sort,' said Rupert, handing Lowri a glass of champagne. 'Adam came round to consult us about the cricket bat he's giving Dominic for his birthday, so Sarah insisted he stay for dinner. One extra is never a problem to my wife.'

'You're a lucky man,' said Adam with feeling.

'I second that!' Rupert raised his glass.

Lowri joined in the toast with enthusiasm, then excused herself to go off in search of Sarah, who was running down the stairs, looking her radiant best in a narrow midnight-blue dress. Lowri thanked her for the gift, lifting one shoulder to emphasise how good the butterfly looked on her dress.

'I thought it would. I helped Rupert choose it. I suppose you know we've got an extra guest?' added Sarah warily as they went into the kitchen together.

'Yes—shall I lay another place?'

'I've already done it. Do you *mind* having Adam here, Lowri?'

'Of course not. Besides, Madam Hostess, it's your dinner party. The guest-list is nothing to do with me.'

'Oh dear. You do mind.' Sarah sighed. 'I didn't ring the flat to tell you in case a mysterious malaise suddenly struck you down. Are you sure you didn't have a fight with Adam that weekend?'

'He was a bit miffed because I wouldn't go out with him.' Lowri tasted the consomme appreciatively. 'His ego took a blow, that's all.'

'Do him the world of good,' said Sarah callously.

Having an extra man at the table was no drawback to the success of the evening—quite the reverse, Lowri discovered, from her own point of view. Sarah's table was round, which made for ease of both seating and conversation, and placed between Tom Harvey and Patrick Savage, a fellow writer friend of Rupert's, with Adam directly opposite, Lowri settled down to enjoy herself rather more than she'd expected.

Far from being glum about his newly divorced state, Tom Harvey seemed in a mood to celebrate it, and proved so entertaining Lowri forgot his renowned intellect in simple enjoyment of his conversation. Patrick Savage, too, was an easy dinner partner, though his conversation, to Lowri's amusement, centred more on his newly born son and small daughter than literature. They chatted comfortably about babies, Lowri telling him about the new arrival due in her own family, and the pleasure she took in Dominic and Emily's company. The blond, attractive man was so engrossed in the subject that she looked up at one point to find Adam's eyes fixed on her in deep disapproval. He turned away instantly to talk to Carey Savage, Patrick's wife, and Lowri quelled a very human little gush of satisfaction as she plunged back into discussion of Rupert's book with Tom Harvey.

When the men returned to the drawing-room later Adam detached Lowri the moment she'd finished handing round coffee. He drew a couple of chairs up near the cool breeze coming in from the windows and installed her in one firmly.

'Neat. Just like one man and his dog,' she commented.

Adam laughed. 'Which one am I?'

'Oh, the man,' said Lowri promptly. 'I'm the nice woolly sheep the dog cuts out from the rest of the flock.'

'A wonder I'm not the dog. Lord knows I'm in the doghouse where you're concerned.'

'Nonsense,' she said lightly, and smiled up at Rupert in refusal as he offered her brandy.

'I won't either,' said Adam with regrets. 'If I'd known I was staying to dinner I'd have come by cab.'

'You're law-abiding, then,' said Lowri, as Rupert moved on to another group of guests.

'Too much at stake for me to be otherwise.' Adam drank his coffee and put their cups down on a nearby table. 'Soon I'll be in the driving seat at Hawk Electronics. My parents are off on a world cruise and I'll be left minding the baby.'

'But this baby is just your cup of tea—far more than the usual kind, I fancy.'

Adam smiled at her. 'Frankly, yes. I know where I am with electronics. Hand me a real live squalling baby and I'd run a mile.' He paused. 'I would have rung you last weekend, but Rupert said you were away.'

Why had he wanted to ring her? 'Yes,' she said serenely. 'I went down to Cwmderwen once Rupert's manuscript was on Tom Harvey's desk.'

Adam's face darkened. 'You were getting on remarkably well with Harvey.'

'Yes—though I've never met him before. He's a very interesting man.'

'And only recently loosed from the chains of matrimony. Be careful, Lowri.'

'I make it a habit to be, Adam,' she said sweetly, and got up. 'Forgive me, I must circulate.'

For the rest of the evening Lowri took good care to avoid privacy with Adam. It was by no means difficult, since Tom Harvey seemed to have taken a fancy to her, and, just as Sarah had predicted, was only too happy to discuss the autumn launch of Rupert's novel all night. It was well after midnight before the party showed any signs of breaking up, and Tom was last to go. Adam, to Lowri's intense disappointment, had been first to leave. Going on somewhere else, of course, she thought in secret fury.

Brenda had left the kitchen spick and span and gone off on the back of her Wayne's motorcycle by the time Lowri said goodnight to Sarah and Rupert.

'Did you have a good time?' asked Rupert, putting an arm round his wife. 'You were talking nineteen to the dozen with Tom Harvey.'

'He's nice. Not so frightening after all,' admitted Lowri.

'How about Adam?' asked Sarah. 'I saw you talking together at one stage.'

Lowri nodded. 'He seemed rather irritated because I got on so well with Tom Harvey.' She exchanged a little smile with Sarah, then said goodnight and left them to lock up as she crossed the moonlit garden to her flat. As she reached the flight of wrought-iron stairs leading to it a figure emerged from the shadows, startling her.

'It's me, Adam,' said the familiar, velvet voice as he moved out into the moonlight.

She breathed out audibly. 'I thought you'd left.'

'I did. But I decided to wait for you, so I walked round and let myself in by the side gate.'

'I was just coming to lock it.'

'Talk to me for a while first.'

'Why?'

'Does there have to be a reason?' he said irritably.

'You must have some reason for coming back at this time of night,' she pointed out.

'I came back to see you. Which,' he added harshly, 'you know perfectly well.'

Lowri battled for a moment with common sense, and lost. 'Then you'd better come up. I'll make coffee.'

He followed her up the stairs with alacrity, eyeing her face as she switched on the lights in her flat.

'I don't want any coffee,' he said bluntly.

Lowri gave him a very straight look. 'Coffee's the only thing on offer.'

'You think I don't know that? I'd decided I just wasn't going to bother again,' he said morosely. 'But one look at you tonight changed all that.' He looked at her slowly, feature by feature. 'Your hair's grown a lot since I first met you. I like it. And you looked so full of life tonight; your eyes shone like lamps when you were talking to Harvey. What the hell was he saying to switch you on like that?'

'We were merely discussing Rupert's book.' Lowri sat down in the adjustable chair at her desk, waving him to the small sofa. 'Won't you sit down?'

Adam shook his head. 'I shan't stay. Not,' he added bitterly, 'that you've any intention of asking me to. Hell, it's so hard not to put a foot wrong. Though it would make it a bloody sight easier if I knew how to put a foot right where you're concerned. I don't usually have this trouble with women.'

'Which says it all, Adam.' Lowri's eyes held his. 'As I said before, I don't want my name on any list of Hawkridge cast-offs.'

'Even if there were a list, which I deny, that wasn't what I had in mind.' He frowned, eyeing her belligerently. 'Can't we just be friends? Looking at you tonight, it suddenly dawned on me why I enjoy your company, why you're so different from the rest.'

'I believe you said something about sexual chemistry,' she said distantly.

'There is that, yes,' he said, pacing up and down restlessly. 'But there's a lot more, too. The other girls I know get bored so easily, but boredom doesn't seem to exist where you're concerned. You enjoy life whatever you're doing, playing cricket with Dom or reading to Emily, working for Rupert or enjoying an evening like tonight. You're involved all the time. It's refreshing, and I like it a lot.'

Lowri looked at him thoughtfully, undecided whether his statement was the simple truth, or some new line he was casting after the one who got away.

'What, exactly,' she began slowly, 'do you mean by "friends"?'

Scenting victory, Adam turned the full battery of his smile on her. 'I want to share my final fling of freedom with you, Lowri. I could get tickets to any show you fancy, take you to Ascot, Wimbledon, Henley.' The familiar gleam danced in his eyes. 'I'll even throw in a test match at Lords.'

Lowri looked at him in silence for a long time. How damnably attractive he was, she thought hopelessly. She'd been doing so well until tonight, too. And just one look at him had been enough to have her hooked again, utterly and completely. It didn't matter whether he took her to Ascot or Lords or just stayed here in her little room with her all the time they were together, she realised in self-revelation. What mattered was just being with Adam, and if this final fling of his meant he wanted to be her lover, then so be it. It was what she wanted too, if she were honest. She knew his reputation, he'd made no bones about being averse to commitment, but suddenly it seemed silly to deprive herself of a summer idyll she knew would never come her way again.

'Temptation indeed,' said Lowri, at last. She smiled at him whimsically. 'What woman could resist such blandishments?'

'You mean you like the idea?' said Adam, starting towards her.

Lowri held up a hand. 'Wait a minute. Clarify. While you're indulging in these wholesome activities with me, would you also be out partying with Caroline and Co.?'

He shrugged. 'Not if it's an obstacle to your agreement.' He smiled wryly. 'There's been precious little partying lately, anyway—until tonight. My usual social round seems to have lost its charm. In the end I gave up trying to kid myself and called round this evening in the hope of seeing you. The cricket bat was just a flimsy excuse. My hopes rose when I was invited to dinner, but I hardly saw anything of you during the evening. So I came back.'

'So you did.'

They looked at each other for a moment.

'It's a deal then?' said Adam at last, and held out his hand. Lowri got up and shook the hand gravely.

'Deal.' She smiled. 'Would you like that coffee now?'

And suddenly they were back to the day of the picnic, easy with each other as Adam watched her make coffee in her cupboard of a kitchen, talking about his company and how life would be very different for him once his father abdicated.

'That's his word for it,' he explained as they sat down together. 'My mother's always teasing him about giving up his crown.'

'Sarah says your mother's lovely,' said Lowri.

'Sarah's right, even if it is conceited to say so. I'm supposed to be exactly like her.' He scorched her with the hot gold gaze. 'Especially about the eyes.'

Lowri shook her head. 'You just can't help it, can you?'

'Help what?' he demanded innocently.

'You know perfectly well, so stop it.'

Adam grinned. 'All right.' He drank his coffee in one swallow. 'Tell me what happens with you now Rupert's book is finished.'

'I'm already researching the next one.' Lowri chuckled ruefully. 'Which isn't as easy as I thought. I get so involved in what I'm reading I forget to take notes.' She yawned suddenly, and Adam jumped to his feet.

'I've kept you up too late.'

'Not to worry. I get a lovely, lazy lie-in on Sundays.' Lowri stood up, smiling, and held out her hand. 'Goodnight.'

Adam took the hand and bent to kiss her on both cheeks. 'Goodnight. Come down and lock the gate after me to avoid any further nocturnal visitors.'

'You only got in tonight because it was left open for Wayne to collect Brenda on his Harley,' explained Lowri, her cheeks hot from the casual caress.

By the time she'd explained the identity of Brenda and Wayne they were at the gate in the wall. Adam paused, looking down at her in the moonlight.

'I'm glad I yielded to impulse and came back.'

'So am I,' said Lowri honestly.

'Can I take you out to lunch tomorrow?'

'All right. The weather forecast's good. I fancy some fresh air, so my turn to provide the picnic this time.'

CHAPTER SIX

SOMETIMES, when Lowri looked back on the hectic period with Adam, it seemed as though the sun always shone and she was always happy, except for the niggling uncertainty about Adam's feelings. She was never sure whether he was sincerely attracted to her, or merely thought of her as the Clares' little cousin, a playmate whose obvious crush on him was entertaining to indulge. One thing he made very clear was that their weekend expeditions into the country together would have bored his other playmates rigid.

'Playmates!' snorted Lowri as he drove her back from a perfect day in the Cotswolds.

'Just a term to show that none of them meant anything more than a decorative companion for the evening,' he explained. 'The only thing any of the recent ones had in common with you was their single status.'

'Ah! No married ladies?'

Adam shook his head. 'Only one. I avoided citation in a divorce case by the skin of my teeth.' He grimaced. 'Never again.'

Lowri glowered at him. 'I must be mad to associate with a rake like you! You were born in the wrong century—I can just picture you as a Regency buck, gambling and carousing and cuckolding husbands.'

Adam turned indignant eyes on her for a moment. 'It was only one husband—and you can hardly call a bet at Ascot a passion for gambling. Besides, I work damned hard for my living, remember.'

Lowri subsided. 'I'll grant you that.'

'Thank you. And, just for the record, I don't think of *you* as a playmate.'

'Good. I don't look the part.'

'Stop putting yourself down!' he said, exasperated. 'I think you're cute.'

'*Cute*!' she exploded.

'So how would you like me to describe you?'

Lowri thought about it as they reached the Chiswick flyover. 'Interesting? Good company?'

'Both of those,' he agreed, and gave her a sidelong glance. 'And hellish sexy, too, in those shorts.'

She blushed to the roots of her windblown black hair, utterly silenced.

'Cat got your tongue?'

'No one's ever called me sexy before,' she muttered.

'How can you possibly know?' said Adam, grinning. 'Men don't always come out with their private thoughts. Good thing, too,' he added with feeling, thinking it over.

Lowri tugged surreptitiously at the denim shorts, wishing they exposed rather less of her tanned thighs.

'I shouldn't bother,' advised Adam. 'You're only calling my attention to those parts of you I've been panting to touch all afternoon.'

Lowri glared at him. 'You're deliberately trying to embarrass me!'

'Not at all. I was stating the simple truth.'

She breathed in deeply, eyeing his profile with disquiet.

'Do me a favour, Lowri,' he said, exasperated. 'Stop behaving like a virgin sacrifice waiting for the knife! I promise you're safe as houses—at least until we're out of this blasted traffic. The entire population of Britain seems to be converging on London.'

Adam drove the rest of the way to St John's Wood whistling through his teeth with a nonchalance which set Lowri's nerves on edge. When they arrived at the house she unlocked the side gate and marched up the stairs to her flat, leaving Adam to follow her with Sarah's picnic basket, borrowed for the day.

When she'd unlocked her door she put out her hand for the basket, but Adam shook his head.

'No point in telling me you're busy this evening, because I know the Clares are away for the weekend. I'll take you out to supper.'

'I'm not hungry,' lied Lowri.

Adam laughed down at her. 'Is all this maidenly panic because I said I wanted to touch? Lowri, sweetheart, we've had a perfect day out in the sunshine among some of the most beautiful scenery in the country. I looked at your shiny nose and untidy hair as we lay on that hill counting sheep, and I was so pleased with life I suddenly thought how it would crown the day if I took you in my arms and gave you a hug and a kiss. But I didn't. Because I know damn well that if I put a foot wrong again you'll shut yourself up in your little retreat here, and I won't be able to do a damn thing about it because you're safe on Rupert's property.'

Lowri looked at him uncertainly, then suddenly her sense of humour came to the rescue, and she chuckled. 'Sorry! I'm an idiot.'

'True,' agreed Adam, 'but a very *cute* idiot, Lowri Morgan.' He ducked as she aimed a punch at him, then dumped the picnic basket and caught her to him, her flailing arms imprisoned at her sides as he looked deep into her eyes, all the banter suddenly missing. 'Would it be such a death blow to friendship if we did exchange a kiss?'

Despite a strong conviction that it would, Lowri hadn't the will to say no. As his mouth met hers her lips parted in such instinctive response that she felt Adam stiffen against her. Without taking his lips from hers he reached out behind her and opened the door, then lifted her by the elbows and carried her inside. He set her on her feet and stared down at her, breathing unevenly.

Lowri thrust a hand through her hair, gave him a wobbly, shy smile, then she was back in Adam's arms as he kissed her again.

'Might as well be hung for a sheep as a lamb,' he muttered against her mouth and pulled her down on his lap on the sofa, his hand stroking the smooth brown skin of her thigh as he went on kissing her with such undisguised pleasure that she was utterly disarmed. He raised his head a fraction and saw the astonishment in her eyes.

'Any minute now,' he said hoarsely, 'you're bound to throw me out and tell me to get lost again. So while you're still struck dumb I'll make the most of it.' He thrust his hands into her hair and kept her head still as he kissed her with such unexpectedly clumsy ardour that Lowri couldn't control her response. Here was something very different from the smooth, practised lover she'd expected, and somehow it made him all the more dangerous. A good thing, she thought, dazed, that he had no idea that this was what she'd yearned for all along. And now it was happening she didn't want it to stop. Which was where the real danger lay. If Adam really set out to breach her defences he'd find out she didn't have any at all where he was concerned.

When he raised his head at last she stared up at him mutely.

'I thought you'd be blacking my eye by now,' he whispered.

She cleared her throat, heat rushing to her face at the look he gave her.

'I'm surprised you're not.' His mouth twisted wryly. 'The usual Hawkridge finesse went right out of the window.'

'I don't know what that's like but I don't think I'd prefer it,' she said honestly.

His eyes blazed. 'In that case——' He bent his head and ran his tongue over the contours of her lips before suddenly crushing them with a hunger which made her tremble. His arms tightened in a rib-threatening grip but after a while he freed one hand to stroke her thighs again. His long fingers moved upward slowly to find the curves of her breasts, but when he began undoing her shirt buttons in smooth, rapid succession she stiffened and drew away.

'Now that *was* practised,' she said tartly, and slid off his lap, doing up her shirt again.

Adam locked his hands behind his dishevelled head, his teasing eyes gleaming. 'Lowri, I'm a lot older than you, and I've knocked around the world a bit. I'd be lying if I said I hadn't undone a fair few buttons and quite a lot more than that. I like women, and I revel in making love to them, but I make sure that in the process none of them suffer by it, mentally or physically. So my only apology is for letting the sheer pleasure of having you respond so unexpectedly turn me into a crass amateur, like a schoolboy who's never kissed a girl before.'

'That's a long speech,' said Lowri sedately. 'Would you like some more coffee?'

'I'd rather take you to bed.'

She stared at him, startled. 'You don't beat around the bush!'

'Normally there's none to beat around.'

'You mean you'd have already made it to bed by now with anyone else.'

Adam nodded, utterly matter-of-fact. 'Yes. You're the exception.'

'Really?' She got up and took their cups into the kitchen, Adam following behind. 'I like that.'

'Being an exception?'

'Yes.'

Adam shrugged wryly. 'Not that it would have progressed further anyway—at least not tonight.'

'Why, exactly?'

He rubbed his nose, eyeing her warily. 'Because of the nature of our relationship, Lowri, I didn't come prepared for such a contingency.' He smiled as colour flooded her sunburnt face again. 'And somehow I don't think you pop your little Pill like the other girls do.'

Lowri gave him a taunting look over her shoulder as she filled the kettle. 'You're wrong, actually.'

Adam stared in such shock that she swallowed a giggle as she spooned coffee into their cups. 'Are you telling me that all this maidenly reluctance on your part was a front, Lowri?'

'The reluctance, no. But if you mean have I had a lover the answer's yes.' She scowled at him. 'What's so funny about that? I'm twenty-one soon, Adam. A decade or so behind you, of course, but still a bit long in the tooth for maidenly purity.'

He shrugged, his eyes blank. 'I don't know, I just assumed you were——'

'A virgin,' she finished, resigned.

'Yes. I suppose I did.' Adam took the mug of coffee from her and swallowed some of it so convulsively it burnt his mouth.

Lowri handed him a glass of cold water. 'Here. I wouldn't have told you if I'd thought you'd be so shocked.'

'Surprised, not shocked.' His bright eyes narrowed under knitted brows. 'So why have you been handing out the touch-me-not routine?'

'My limited experience has rather made me wary.' She gave him a wry little smile. 'Pity I blurted the truth. I think you'd have been happier if I'd kept it to myself.'

He smiled, suddenly very much in command again. 'Pointless, Lowri. I'd have found out the moment I made love to you. Which I'm going to, I warn you,' he caught her in his arms, 'one day—or night—*very* soon, Lowri Morgan.' He kissed her long and hard before releasing her so suddenly she rocked on her heels. He smiled down at her victoriously. 'But I can be surprisingly patient when I want to be. Sweet dreams, darling. Come and lock the gate after me. If you must stay here alone tonight I want you safe and sound behind locked doors before I leave.'

In bed later Lowri cursed herself for shying away from Adam at the crucial moment. She was so much in love with him by now that she longed for him with an almost physical ache. She tossed and turned, forcing herself to face the truth. As she'd told Adam, it wouldn't be the first time. And last time she'd been hurt. She knew she would be this time, too, when it ended, but in a very different way. Adam was utterly honest about his no-strings, non-commitment policy. Philip Garfield had conned her from the first.

When Philip had been seconded from London to the Newport office, Lowri, knowing she was the envy of her female colleagues, had been utterly dazzled by the clever, confident man who'd pursued her openly from the moment they met. He flattered and courted Lowri, taking her out to dinner and the theatre, and finally away to a remote little hotel in mid-Wales for a secret, romantic weekend, with veiled promises of an important question to ask. Convinced Philip meant to propose, an excited Lowri had rushed off to what she believed was her destiny. In actual fact Philip had taken her to bed the moment they arrived, stampeding her swiftly and disappointingly into her first encounter with what she recognised instantly as mere sex and nothing to do with love. The moment it was over Philip confessed he was married. He told a shattered Lowri that he was separated from the wife who refused to divorce him. But for the brief period of his secondment there was no reason why he and his darling little Lowri couldn't enjoy a nice, intimate little relationship, as long as they were discreet.

Lowri, furious and disillusioned told him exactly what he could do with his neat little plan, repacked her bag and hitchhiked home to Cwmderwen. Life was one long, dull torture for a while afterwards as she came in contact with Philip Garfield daily at work. He made a very public show of ignoring her completely, giving rise to all kinds of comments from her colleagues, but Lowri hid her humiliation, refused to rise when she was teased, and greeted news of her subsequent redundancy with euphoria.

With Adam it was different. She was going into this with her eyes wide open, willing to share his final fling and prepared to cut her losses when responsibility finally overtook him. Or even sooner if he got tired of her first—or she of him. Lowri gave a mirthless little laugh in the darkness. Who are you kidding? She asked herself. You'll never tire of Adam if you live to a hundred.

All next day, through the flurry of welcome when the Clares returned, and the time she spent typing the notes she'd made about life in the fourteenth-century reign of Edward III, Lowri waited, strung tight as a violin string, for Adam to ring. When he did it was so late she'd given up all hope of hearing from him, and gave him a cool response.

'I've only just got back to the flat—sorry it's late, Lowri. Hope you aren't in bed.'

'No. I've been over at the house, chatting to Sarah.'

'I detect a hint of frost.'

'Certainly not.'

'Good. I would have rung earlier, but I spent most of the day with Dad and the rest of the board. Things are hotting up now his retirement's looming closer.'

'And at your age you must get tired so easily!' she said, mock solicitous.

'You little devil,' he hissed. 'If I had you right here in my arms this minute I'd show you exactly how old and tired I am!'

The laughing intimacy in the deep, caressing voice tightened muscles Lowri wasn't usually much aware of.

'No response?' he asked, amused.

'Yes. But I'm not telling you what it is,' she said demurely, and heard a sharp intake of breath.

'Witch! When can I see you again? Tonight?'

Summoning all her willpower, Lowri tried to postpone seeing him for a couple of days just to convince herself she was in control, but Adam wouldn't hear of it, telling her bluntly he intended to spend as much of his free time with her as he possibly could.

'You're seeing quite a bit of Adam these days,' said Sarah a couple of days later. 'He's staying the course with you far longer than he usually does with the Carolines of this world.'

'Probably because we're just friends,' said Lowri, not altogether truthfully.

'Or maybe because you're the only one who's ever held out against the famous Hawkridge charm.' Sarah eyed her young cousin challengingly. 'I take it you *are* holding out?'

Lowri grinned. 'Since you ask, yes. I am.'

'I'm amazed. Rupert says——'

'You and Rupert discuss me?'

'Of course we do! We're not just fond of you—we feel responsible, too.'

'Oh, Sarah!' Lowri blinked hard.

'Now don't go all mushy and sentimental on me, but it's the truth just the same,' Sarah pulled a face. 'I wouldn't put it past Rupert to corner Adam and demand his intentions!'

'He'd better not!' said Lowri in alarm, then shrugged. 'Besides, I know exactly what Adam's intentions are—a good time, no strings and no recriminations when we go our separate ways.'

Sarah snorted. 'He doesn't want much, does he? Are you happy with that?'

'Yes,' fibbed Lowri firmly. 'Adam's great fun, and I enjoy his company, but he's the last man I'd think of settling down with. When I get to that stage—which won't be for years yet—I'll find me a man who doesn't run a mile at the thought of commitment and babies.'

It was a thought which sustained her through dinner at an Italian restaurant in Putney the following Friday, an outing to seventeenth-century Ham House near the Thames below Richmond Hill the day after, right through an evening at the theatre watching the new Tom Stoppard play and up to the moment when Adam saw her through the Clares' side gate late on the Saturday night. At the foot of her stair Lowri stood firm, baulking any attempt on Adam's part to see her inside the flat.

'You're not letting me come up tonight,' he stated wryly. 'Is that because the family's in residence over at the house this weekend?'

Lowri thought about it, and nodded. 'I rather think it is.' It was the truth. Inviting Adam to share a bed which actually belonged to the Clares didn't seem the right thing to do. She reached up a hand to his face. 'You probably think I'm silly.'

'No—just very, very sweet.' Adam kissed the hand and held it tight. 'How about tomorrow? The weekend isn't over yet.'

'Right. Where do you want to go?'

'I thought a swim and a picnic—my turn to provide the eats.'

Lowri nodded happily. 'Sounds lovely. Where?'

Adam grinned. 'Wait and see.' He bent swiftly and kissed her gently. Then kissed her again, less gently, and suddenly they were locked in each others' arms careless of the fact that they were in full view of anyone who cared to stroll in the garden in the scented, summer darkness.

Adam put her from him at last, breathing hard. 'I'd better go,' he said unevenly.

She nodded wordlessly, reached up for one last kiss, then went inside her little flat and shut the door before she could change her mind.

Adam had been gone for half an hour before it suddenly dawned on Lowri that the only decent swimsuit she possessed was at home in Cwmderwen. Swimming hadn't featured in her life since her arrival in London.

'No problem,' said Sarah cheerfully next day over the lazy, once-weekly ritual of breakfast Lowri usually shared with the Clares. 'You can borrow one of mine.'

'It wouldn't fit,' said Lowri, depressed.

'Rubbish. I'm not the sylph I was since Emily's advent, and you've lost a few pounds lately, I fancy.'

'Am I working you too hard, Lowri?' demanded Rupert, emerging from a screen of Sunday papers suddenly.

'No, of course not.'

'I don't want Geraint on the rampage because I'm wearing his daughter to a shadow!'

'If anyone's wearing her to a shadow, darling, it's Adam, not you,' said his wife.

'Geraint might not be too pleased about that, either,' he said darkly, and eyed Lowri in suspicion. 'Everything all right?'

'Of course it is. Adam's just a friend, Rupert.'

'Hmm.' Rupert retreated behind his paper, unconvinced, and Sarah took Lowri upstairs to choose something for the swimming expedition.

Firmly rejecting brief two-piece trifles Sarah offered her, Lowri seized on a plain, beautifully cut black one-piece maillot which flattered her shape very satisfactorily and showed off the tan she'd acquired during lunchbreaks spent lying in the recent sunshine they'd been blessed with.

When Adam arrived to collect her it was an hour before they got away, due to offers of coffee from Sarah, and pleas to stay from Emily and Dominic. When they heard he was taking Lowri swimming, the longing on both young faces prompted a promise from Adam that he'd include them both in the next swimming expedition.

'But not today,' said Adam, as he drove Lowri away later. 'Today I want you all to myself.'

Smiling happily in agreement, Lowri asked where they were headed.

'You'll see soon enough,' he said mysteriously. 'I hope you've brought something to swim in.'

Lowri assured him she had and sat back, letting her hair blow in the wind, her face to the sun as Adam's roadster took her through London on the way to the mysterious destination. When they eventually arrived she stared in surprise as he drove into the underground car park of a large block of flats.

'Why are we stopping here?'

'Because this is where we're going swimming, my pet.' Adam grinned at her as he switched off the ignition. 'Wapping, home of rising young electronics wizard Adam Hawkridge.'

Lowri stared at him, then began to laugh. 'I'd rather expected Brighton.'

'Too unoriginal. You'll like it much better here in Wapping.'

He was right. The indoor swimming-pool attached to the building was a surprisingly luxurious affair, with pillars and concealed lighting, greenery in tubs, and not another soul in sight.

'Where is everyone?' asked Lowri later, when she emerged in her borrowed bathing suit.

'In bed—or in Brighton, probably,' said Adam with a grin, and gave her a swift, all-encompassing scrutiny from head to foot. 'Very nice indeed, Miss Morgan.'

'Likewise, Mr Hawkridge,' she returned serenely, her colour a little high. But impressive was more the word, she thought secretly, one swift look enough for an indelible impression of broad shoulders and slim hips, long, muscular legs. And without any fuss she dived neatly into the water and set out for the far end with the efficient crawl she'd learned at school. Adam dived in after her and passed her without effort, treading water until she joined him, then turned with her to swim effortlessly at her pace for several lengths before suddenly disappearing beneath the water. She looked about her nonplussed for a moment, then suddenly Adam shot up out of the water, imprisoning her in his arms, laughing. Just as abruptly he let her go again, and for a few minutes they ducked and dived and splashed like children, before Lowri took off at the fastest speed she could manage, only to be caught long before she reached the far end of the pool.

'All right, all right,' she gasped. 'You win.'

Adam heaved himself out of the water and leant down to pull her up out the water in one easy movement, not even short of breath as he wrapped her in her pink towelling robe.

'That was fun,' she said breathlessly, rubbing her hair with a sleeve. 'So where do we go for the picnic?'

'Not far. You don't even have to change first. Just bring your bag with you and we can go up in the service lift as we are.'

Lowri eyed him narrowly. 'You mean you're taking me to your flat?'

He nodded, grinning from ear to ear. 'Bullseye. If you're *very* good I may even show you my etchings.'

Adam's home was high up in the modern, pyramid-shaped building, with a bird's eye view of the Thames from the terrace outside his living room. It was a white-walled, sparsely furnished place, a very masculine air about its stripped wood floors, and furniture covered in glove-soft Italian leather the colour of vintage port. The windows had louvred blinds instead of curtains, and the only wall free of bookshelves was hung with a variety of artwork ranging from a pair of small oils to a series

of pen and ink sketches. Adam's kitchen was clinically
white and businesslike, but his bathroom had a touch
of the sybarite about the coral-red walls and black and
white chequered floor, the claw-footed Victorian bathtub
and huge gold-framed mirror sporting cherubs at each
corner.

'Gosh,' said Lowri, awed. 'So this is how the man-
about-town lives.'

'Only very recently,' he assured her. 'I still have my
bedroom at home with my parents. And after that and
before this—when I came home from the States—I had
a rather scruffy place not far from here in a less up-
wardly mobile part of the community.' He indicated a
pile of striped black and white towels on a wooden stand
the same vintage as the bath. 'Help yourself—plenty of
shampoo and so on. I'll get lunch ready.'

'Don't you need a hand?'

'Not for my type of catering!'

Lowri had a swift bath, washed her hair free of
chlorine and dried it vigorously on one of the huge
towels. Afterwards she added a touch of colour to her
lips, flicked on some mascara and resumed the yellow
cotton dress she'd worn earlier. When she emerged, damp
hair caught back from her face with a yellow towelling
bandeau, Adam was in the kitchen, wearing a fresh white
cotton shirt and jeans, his bare feet in espadrilles and
his hair still damp.

He looked up with a smile. 'I hope you're not allergic
to lobster.'

'Only to the cost,' she assured him.

Adam led her to a glass-topped table on the small
terrace, seated her in a red leather chair and served her
half a lobster with lemon mayonnaise, crisp green salad
and hot Italian bread. They drank dry white wine with
the meal, then took a rest for a while before Adam
produced a Sachertorte frosted in smooth dark chocolate too alluring for Lowri to resist.

'Catering's easy if one patronises a certain well-known chain-store foodhall,' said Adam, grinning. 'A half-hour shopping session yesterday morning before I came for you and hey presto, lunch for two.'

'It was wonderful,' said Lowri with a sigh, gazing out at the Thames.

'Would you like some coffee?'

'Not at the moment.' Lowri slid lower in the chair. 'I just want to sit in the sunshine and gaze at the view for a while. I'll help you wash up later.'

'No need. I've got a machine for that.'

Lowri chuckled. 'Have you got a machine for everything?'

'No,' said Adam softly. 'Some things a machine can't do for a man.'

She shot him a look, but his bright eyes were bland beneath the thick straight brows.

'Adam,' she said bluntly. 'Is this the one day soon you were talking about? Have you brought me here to seduce me?'

He threw back his head and laughed. 'When it comes to a bush you don't beat around it much yourself, Lowri Morgan.'

She took off the bandeau and shook out her hair to dry in the sunshine. 'You must admit this has all the hallmarks—the surprise trip to your flat, the exquisite meal, the wine. The works, in fact.'

Adam got up to collect plates. 'You've forgotten something I once told you, Lowri. I only take what's freely given. Does that answer your question?'

'I don't know.' She yawned, suddenly sleepy after the swim and the wine and the sunshine. 'I'll think about it.'

'You just sit there while I see to this lot. When I come back you can tell me exactly how you'd like to spend the rest of the day.'

She nodded drowsily. 'Right.' When she was alone Lowri relaxed completely, only dimly aware of the drone of traffic somewhere in the distance below. Her eyelids felt weighted, and soon all her thought processes ground to a halt and she fell asleep.

Lowri woke with a start, disorientated, to find herself on a wide bed in cool twilight in what was obviously Adam's bedroom. A swift look at her watch told her it wasn't late evening, as it might well have been from the light. It was a mere three hours since lunch. She shot upright in dismay. Taking a long nap—or any nap at all—was hardly good manners for a guest invited to lunch. She slid off the bed rapidly, opened the blinds and went into Adam's bathroom to spend a few necessary minutes there. Her bag, she saw, touched, had been left by the side of the bed where she would find it easily. After a touch of lipstick and a vigorous session with her hairbrush she went in search of Adam to apologise.

He was out on the terrace, deep in the Sunday papers. As she stepped out from the living-room he jumped to his feet, smiling.

'Better?' He ran his eyes over her. 'You look all flushed and rested—good enough to eat.'

'I've slept for ages. I'm very sorry,' she said penitently.

'Why?' He held out a chair for her. 'I'm flattered you felt at home enough here to relax.'

'I don't imagine women usually fall asleep on you,' she said drily.

He grinned. 'Not over lunch, anyway.'

Lowri flushed. 'I'd quite like that coffee now.'

'Coming up,' he said promptly. 'Or you can have tea, if you like.'

'Oh, yes, please! Shall I——?'

'No. You just sit there and read the paper.'

When Adam brought a tea tray he'd added a plate of cookies. 'I thought you'd like something to nibble with the tea—all from the same reliable source.'

'I know. They're my favourites.'

They drank tea together, ate a few cookies, talked about some of the news items Adam picked out from the paper. Then Lowri flipped through the pages of the magazine, showing him several pages of the latest beachwear.

'None of them comes within streets of that black affair you were wearing,' said Adam.

'Borrowed plumes from Sarah. Mine's at home.'

'Wherever it came from, you looked good in it. Very good,' he added with emphasis.

'It must be the cut.'

'No, sweetheart, it was the shape inside it.'

Adam's eyes met hers, and held, and at last she looked away, seizing on the book review section from the pile of papers in front of her. She studied it furiously, suddenly so intensely aware of the man beside her the paper shook in her hands.

Adam cleared his throat. 'We'd better go out,' he said gruffly and got up, holding out his hand to her. 'Come on, we'll go for a drive, walk in a park somewhere.'

Lowri nodded blindly and dropped the paper, then bent to pick it up just as Adam did the same. Their heads cracked together and she gave a little shriek and Adam caught her in his arms and held her close.

'Darling, did I hurt you?'

Lowri shook her head.

'Look at me,' he ordered. 'Look at me, Lowri!'

Slowly, reluctantly, her lids lifted until she met the question in his intent, brilliant eyes. She answered it without words, melting against him, rubbing her cheek against his chest, and Adam picked her up and carried her through his living-room and along the hall, with a slow, measured tread like a sleepwalker, giving her every opportunity to change her mind right up to the moment when he lowered her to his bed and stretched himself out beside her.

They lay face to face, as still as their mutual, thundering heartbeat allowed, then Adam bent his head and Lowri met his kiss with a fire which dispensed with questions. The spell abruptly broken, they surged together, hands and lips seeking and urgent, and at last, breathing laboured, Adam took off her clothes with unsteady hands rendered clumsy by need. As before, Lowri's response to such lack of skill was so heated that Adam tore off his own clothes and pulled her naked body close, his breath leaving his lungs with a rush at the contact. Hard, muscular angles and soft, buoyant curves fitted together with such exquisite exactitude that Lowri's hips moved involuntarily and Adam gave a smothered sound, his kisses suddenly famished and desperate as he caressed her to a fever-pitch of longing. And at last, vanquished by the need overwhelming them both, he buried his face against her throat and their bodies flowed together in such harmony that there on a sunny Sunday afternoon, high above the Thames, they achieved a miracle that for Adam with all his experience, and for Lowri with virtually none, was as near perfection as two humans could ever hope to achieve.

CHAPTER SEVEN

IT WAS almost dawn when Adam drove Lowri back to St John's Wood.

'I'm glad it's so late,' she said drowsily. 'I don't want to run into Sarah or Rupert—or anyone in the world tonight.'

Adam ran a caressing hand over her thigh. 'Why not?'

'Because I rather fancy that what's happened is writ large in my face, Adam Hawkridge. One look at me and Sarah will know how I spent a shamefully major part of my Sunday.'

He gave her a questioning, sidelong glance. 'Regrets, Lowri?'

She thought about it for a moment. 'Theoretically I should have some, I suppose. But I don't. At least I now know what all the fuss is about. I didn't know it could be like that.'

'Neither did I.' He smiled wryly at the disbelieving look she turned on him. 'It's God's truth, Lowri. I've made love to a lot of women. I admit it. But until today I thought of lovemaking as—well as a sort of appetite, like eating your dinner, or enjoying a fine wine. With you it was different. Surely you realised that?'

'It was certainly different for me,' she agreed. 'But my former brush with the subject was a disaster, so almost anything halfway pleasant would have been better.'

'Thanks a lot!' His hand tightened cruelly on her knee. 'Who was he?'

'No point in telling you. You wouldn't know him. And the whole affair finished before it started, almost, when I found out he was married.'

Adam brought the car to a halt near the gate in the Clares' garden wall. 'I'm coming in,' he said brusquely, as he helped her out.

Lowri gave him a startled glance, and without a word unlocked the gate and ran ahead of him up the stairs to her flat. Once inside he took her in his arms and kissed her, and went on kissing her until their hearts were pounding.

'I know it's illogical,' he said through his teeth, 'but after what happened today I can't stand the thought of other men, past or present. I won't share, Lowri.'

'Does that work both ways?' she demanded.

'Of course it does,' he said roughly. 'Rules of the game.' His eyes darkened. 'What the hell is it about you? I want you again, right now.'

Lowri stared at him, her breathing quickening. Colour flooded her face as he caught her to him and began kissing her again, all over her face and down her neck until she pushed him away with shaking hands. 'Adam, I need breathing space. This is all a bit—sudden.'

'Sudden!' He gave a bark of laughter. 'I gave you due warning days ago.'

Her eyes locked with his. 'So was lunch at your place part of an overall plan for what happened?'

Adam's eyes gleamed irrepressibly. 'Of course it was. Thoughts of taking you to bed were keeping me awake at night.'

Lowri's eyes softened at his honesty. 'I confess to the odd girlish fantasy on the subject myself.' She smiled a little. 'Not that any of them were a patch on the reality. It's easy to see why all the girls are mad about you.'

He seized her shoulders and shook her. 'Don't cheapen it, Lowri. It's never been like that with anyone else. Nor do I know why it is with you. You're not conventionally pretty or a sensational shape——'

'Like the others,' she snapped.

'Will you stop banging on about the others? Just believe me when I say that our experience together was a rare and beautiful thing. For me, anyway,' he added roughly, and pushed her away.

Lowri pulled him back, sliding her arms round his neck. 'It was for me too—and you know it.'

Adam kissed her long and hard, then released her with reluctance. 'Time I let you go to bed,' he said, touching a hand to her cheek.

'I probably won't sleep.' She gave him a half-embarrassed little smile. 'I've spent too much time in bed today already!'

Sleep soon came last on Lowri's list of priorities, since Adam demanded they spend every possible moment they could together, making no secret of the fact that once he was in charge at the firm his time would no longer be his own.

'We'll still see each other as much as I can manage,' he assured her, 'but it might have to be just weekends for a while until I settle into the new job. But until then,' he said, smiling in a way which made her heart turn over, 'I want to see as much of you as I can, starting right now.'

'Which means get your clothes off and come to bed, I suppose,' said Lowri cheekily, then gave a squeak as he yanked her into his arms and slid down the zip of her dress almost in one movement.

'I'm more than willing to do it for you,' he assured her as they fell, laughing together, on his wide, welcoming bed.

Sarah and Rupert were worried, Lowri knew, but refrained from interference with a tact she deeply appreciated. She told Sarah so when her cousin came up to the office one morning with a covered dish of pasta for Lowri's lunch.

'Whatever it is you do with Adam, it can't include food much,' said Sarah bluntly. 'You're losing weight, and you're all eyes. Can't you sleep?'

'Oh, yes, when I get the chance——' Lowri stopped dead, blushing vividly.

Sarah sighed. 'Go on, eat this up while it's hot. I'll make us some coffee.' She came back with two mugs and perched on the arm of the sofa, eyeing Lowri while she ate.

'You couldn't hold out, then.'

'No.' Lowri met her cousin's beautiful eyes squarely. 'As must be perfectly obvious.'

'Since you mention it, *cariad*, yes, it is.' Sarah hesitated. 'Does your father know?'

'I told him I've got a boyfriend.'

'Is that how you think of Adam?'

Lowri smiled wryly. 'I don't think Dad would appreciate being told I've got a lover. It's such an emotive sort of word.'

'But pretty apt, just the same. You're head over heels in love, aren't you?'

'You know I am. I have been from the moment I first laid eyes on Adam, if we're into truth here.'

'In that case it's a miracle you held out so long!' Sarah examined her fingernails intently. 'How does he feel about you?'

Lowri hesitated. 'It never ceases to amaze me that he wants to take me to bed the minute we're together, if that's what you're asking. And even out of bed we enjoy each other's company. Adam's a lot of fun to be with. But beyond that your guess is as good as mine.'

'Rupert's making noises like an anxious parent, you know.'

'That's very sweet of him. But tell him not to worry. I went into this with my eyes wide open.'

Sarah got up to go. 'Just remember we're here if you want us. Any time at all.'

Lowri smiled. 'Thanks Sarah. By the way, Adam suggests we take Emily and Dominic over to his place on Saturday morning for a swim in the pool, then out somewhere for lunch.'

'Which means straight to the nearest burger bar, of course.' Sarah looked pleased. 'It's very good of Adam— in the circumstances I'm surprised he can spare the time!'

Then to her dismay Lowri caught a stomach bug and had to spend a couple of days in bed, precious time she begrudged away from Adam. Marooned in her bedroom, feeling wretched both from the malaise and the anti-biotics she was given to cure it, Lowri had more cause than ever to feel grateful to Sarah, who looked after her without fussing, and kept Rupert and the children away until the patient was on the mend.

Adam was refused admittance until Lowri felt confident she'd stopped throwing up, but he came to see her the moment he was allowed, complete with flowers and books, and adamant she needed a breath of country air to complete the cure.

'My parents own a cottage a few miles from Hereford,' he told her. 'I'll drive you down there this weekend for some peace and quiet far from the madding crowd.' He sat on the edge of the bed, smiling into her eyes. 'I'm suffering too. It's a hell of a long time since I held you in my arms.'

'You can't want to the way I look now,' she said, slight colour tinging her face.

'Wrong!' And to illustrate his point Adam drew her up against him gently, and kissed her at length. 'I'll come for you on Friday afternoon.'

Lowri recovered as quickly as she'd succumbed. Probably, she told herself, because the prospect of a weekend away with Adam was a more effective cure than all the pills she'd swallowed.

The cottage was a long way from anywhere, reached by an unadopted road which led up past a few isolated houses to a common which stretched for miles with no sign of human habitation.

'Nothing to disturb us here,' said Adam, as he led the way down a steep garden to a cottage with glorious views across a valley from its front windows. 'Peter and I loved it here. He was a lot older than me, but he let me go with him to roam over the common, go shooting for rabbits, pick hops, too, in September. And sometimes we'd sneak out at night and lie low in the garden for hours for a glimpse of the local badger family.'

Lowri gazed at the view with a rapturous sigh, then held out her arms to Adam. 'It's utterly perfect. Thank you for bringing me here.'

He hugged her close, kissed her, then put her away from him firmly. 'Supper first, then an early night. You must be tired.'

Lowri smiled invitingly. 'I'm not in the least tired, but the early night sounds good.'

'If you smile at me like that it'll be earlier than you think,' he warned, grinning. 'Come and help me put supper.'

Later, as they lay together in bed, tired at last after lovemaking all the more impassioned after the period of abstinence, she marvelled at the sheer quiet of the place after London, and stared wistfully into the darkness which was so much more intense here, far away from any city lights. This was such a perfect place for a honeymoon. She knew beyond all doubt that she wanted to belong to Adam for the rest of her life, but if he felt the same way he never said so. He made love to her as though she were food and he starved for her, talked to her on every subject under the sun, and laughed and teased and paid her extravagant compliments. But he never said a word about love. Lowri curved her body closer to his, making a fierce, silent vow to convince Adam once and for all that marriage was their mutual destiny.

Lowri got her wish, but, like the one granted by the monkey's paw, it was in the last form she wanted. After a couple of weeks' panic Lowri secretly bought herself a pregnancy testing kit, got in an even worse panic at the result, and felt sick with apprehension as she went to meet Adam at the flat one Friday night. When he let her in he looked drawn and haggard himself, with dark smudges beneath his eyes, and for once looked every one of the years she teased him about so often. For a moment she was tempted to keep quiet, to wait for another more propitious time. But, afraid there'd never be one, she blurted out the news the moment he'd closed the door behind him.

'You're *what*!' said Adam, his eyes narrowed to appalled slits.

'I'm pregnant,' she repeated baldly.

'How?'

'In the usual way, Adam. With your help,' she added, feeling cold.

He flung away to pace round the room like a caged tiger. 'I suppose you forgot to take your Pill,' he threw at her.

'I did not!' Her eyes flashed. 'I take it religiously, always. But I had a stomach bug, remember. I took antibiotics, and the Pill didn't work this time. It's not infallible.'

Adam stared at her in brooding silence for so long Lowri shivered, despite the warmth of the evening. 'Are you telling me the truth, Lowri?' he said slowly at last. 'Or did you by any chance engineer this little "accident" deliberately, to trap me?'

Lowri's heart gave a sickening thump against her ribs. The silence in the room lengthened again cruelly before she said in a flat, wooden voice, 'No. I didn't do that. I'd better go.' She turned away to pick up her overnight bag.

'Don't be so stupid,' he said brusquely, looking more like a grim stranger than the rakish, laughing Adam she'd fallen in love with. 'We've got some sorting out to do.'

Lowri shook her head, her face blank. 'No. We haven't. You've just made it patently clear I'm to blame. In which case any sorting out is my business, none of yours.' She made for the door without a backward glance, but his hand came down hard on her shoulder before she reached it.

'Lowri, wait.' Adam's tone was slightly more conciliatory. 'I suppose I shouldn't have said that—but hell, surely you can appreciate the shock you gave me. Let's talk things through, go over the options.'

'Options?' She gave him a look of such glacial distaste angry colour rose in Adam's face.

'Yes, options!' he snapped, and forced her down into a chair.

'If you're about to give me the address of a nice private clinic, don't bother,' she flung up at him. 'It might do for your other women, but not for me.'

'None of my so-called "other women" ever put me in this position,' he hurled back, his face white with anger.

'It's the first time for me, too! Do you think I'm enjoying this?' She jumped up, but Adam shoved her back again ungently, then bit his lip, thrusting his hand through his hair.

'Sorry—didn't think.'

'That makes two of us,' snapped Lowri. 'A bit more thought on my part and none of this would be happening.'

'Don't be stupid. It is happening, so something must be done about it,' he said forcefully.

'First,' said Lowri coldly, 'let me make two things very clear. I intend both to have the baby, *and* to keep it.' She gestured at him regally. 'Now you can have your say.'

Adam stared down at her, his eyes oddly blank. 'I see. It's ultimatum time.' He shrugged. 'All right. You leave me with no choice. We get married.'

'Oh, *please*,' she said scathingly. 'Spare me the histrionics. Right from the beginning you made it clear that marriage and a family are the last things you want. Besides, shotgun weddings are a bit out of date, Adam. Please don't trouble yourself. I'll manage on my own.'

'Who's into histrionics now?' Adam's mouth tightened. 'You're being stupid again, Lowri. There's nothing else for it. I'll arrange a quiet wedding as quickly as possible——'

'To hide my shame?' she said derisively. 'Get real, Adam. Times have changed.'

Adam's jaw set. 'It's nothing like that. I meant that we have to get it done quickly before—before my time's taken up with the changeover at Hawk Electronics.'

'Ah, yes, Hawk Electronics—your *real* baby.' Lowri stared blindly at her feet for a long time, her mind working at a furious rate. 'Right,' she said at last. 'But with one proviso.'

He sighed irritably. 'What now?'

'We keep the entire thing, wedding included, secret until it's done. Then to the world a quick, quiet wedding was just our rush to tie the knot before you take over the firm, as you said. But no word about the baby until absolutely necessary.'

Adam looked impatient. 'It's not a secret you can keep for long, Lowri.'

'Long enough to give me—and you—a bit of breathing space; time to adjust to the idea,' said Lowri firmly, and stood up. 'Now I really must go.'

Adam's eyes softened slightly for the first time since she'd broken the news. 'Why? You look exhausted. Anyway, I thought you were staying tonight.'

She gave him a scathing look. 'Bad idea, in the circumstances.'

'I'll sleep on the sofa out here, if you prefer,' he offered.

Lowri stared at him, wondering why a man of his famed experience with women couldn't tell that she yearned for him to take her to bed and hold her in his arms all night. The last thing in the world she needed was a night in his bed alone while he slept on his rotten sofa.

'No, thanks. I'll just ring for a cab——'

'Don't be stupid, I'll drive you,' he snapped angrily.

'If you call me stupid once more I'll hit you, so stop it!' she bit back, cut to pieces because he hadn't insisted she stay.

'I will when you stop talking like an idiot!' He seized her arm to march her through the hall to the door. 'I'm driving you home, whether you want me to or not.'

Afterwards Lowri could never look back on what followed without shuddering. From the moment she broke the unwelcome news Adam changed from a laughing, demanding lover into a humourless, businesslike stranger who condemned her insistence on utter secrecy as both juvenile and irritating.

'Nevertheless I insist,' Lowri said obdurately. 'We can get it over with while your mother and father are away on their cruise.'

'*Your* father's not on a cruise,' Adam pointed out curtly. 'Won't he think it a touch odd when you present me as a *fait accompli* after the deed is done?'

'Dad's very much taken up with his own affairs at the moment,' said Lowri flatly. 'Holly's not too well. No point in adding to his worries.'

Adam eyed her morosely. 'I trust you'll tell him it wasn't my idea when the time comes.'

'Don't worry, I'll take the blame.' Lowri smiled at him disdainfully. 'I'll make *sure* he knows *none* of this was your idea.'

Their relationship changed so completely it was hard sometimes for Lowri to remember Adam as someone she once had fun with, let alone as a demanding lover. To keep the change from Sarah and Rupert, Lowri asked Adam to avoid St John's Wood for the time being.

'Let's keep to neutral ground until—until afterwards,' she said firmly. 'Restaurants will do.'

'Bloody waste of money.' Adam eyed her barely touched dinner grimly. 'You hardly eat anything. We might as well stay at home and have a sandwich—I could save money for my approaching commitments.'

'Perhaps it might be better if we don't meet at all until the wedding,' she said stonily.

'Don't be——' Adam caught himself up in time. 'Look, Lowri, why won't you come back to my place? I promise not to lay a finger on you until after we're married if that's what you want.'

What utter idiots men could be, thought Lowri bitterly. Adam's obvious distaste for laying a finger on her was precisely why she preferred to give his flat a wide berth. News of forthcoming fatherhood had been the kiss of death to his famed libido as far as she was concerned. He gave her impersonal goodnight kisses, it was true, but they were perfunctory gestures unworthy of the word caress. They spent less and less time together as the date of their nuptials approached.

'Might as well get as much work in beforehand as possible,' said Adam in extenuation. 'My parents leave next week, remember. And while we're on the subject I still think you should meet them before they go.'

'No!' Lowri was adamant. 'Let's leave it until they get back.'

One evening, shortly before the date set for the secret wedding, Sarah surprised Lowri in tears, and proceeded to extract the entire story from her, then took her over to the house to repeat it to Rupert. Lowri talked with them into the small hours, glad at last to confide in someone, and feeling it was only fair that they, at least, should know the truth. Her gratitude was boundless when they hugged her close and reiterated their pledge of help and support as they walked her back to the flat through the starlit garden.

The wedding-day dawned as bright and sunny as any bride could wish for. Lowri looked up at the sky with a wry smile, had a bath, washed her hair and dried it carefully, a process which took longer now her hair had grown. She took almost as long over her face, dressed with care, added the last bits and pieces to the luggage waiting near the door. Afterwards she went over to the house and bade a rather emotional farewell to Sarah and Rupert, and hugged Emily hard, grateful that Dominic was playing cricket, and spared the embarrassment of seeing her cry.

When the taxi came she was ready and waiting, her tears dry, and her face composed. With one last round of goodbyes she got in the cab, waving to the others as it moved away, then turned in her seat to stare straight ahead, feeling that one chapter in her life was well and truly over. She hadn't wanted to leave Sarah and Rupert to face the music, but Rupert was adamant. When Adam Hawkridge came storming round to the house, as he was certain to do, not only would he find the bird flown, he'd have Rupert Clare at his most formidable to contend with.

Lowri stared out of the window, feeling no qualms at all about leaving Adam in the lurch. In fact, she discovered, it satisfied some deep, primeval need in her to think of him pacing up and down waiting for the bride who never came. Do him good, she thought fiercely. Who said revenge wasn't sweet? In her mind's eye she could just picture him jamming coins in a callbox to ring her, then driving like a maniac to St John's Wood to pick up the terse letter Rupert had ready and waiting for him.

Dear Adam,
You're saved. My pregnancy was a false alarm, after all. Put it down to panic, or maybe a faulty testing kit. Either way, the hole-and-corner wedding isn't necessary. Not that *I* ever insisted on it. You did—probably afraid it would tarnish your image to be seen as shirking your responsibilities. You've got so many of these now you must be glad of one less. Especially this one.

This is not an apology for standing you up at the register office, by the way. I did that deliberately—my little gesture of retaliation. You were not kind, Adam. And lately you've become a stranger. One I don't want to know any more.
    Goodbye,
    Lowri.

CHAPTER EIGHT

Lowri locked the shop door with a sigh of relief, stretched mightily, then called down the stairs to the basement.

'Everything all right, Jenny?'

'Fine,' came the answer. 'Just tidying up a bit.'

'Could you hang on a few minutes while I nip to the supermarket? We were so busy at lunchtime I never got out to buy food.'

'Take as long as you like, Boss. We're perfectly happy down here. I'm in no hurry.'

'Great. Won't be long.'

Lowri let herself out of the shop, took a quick, proprietary look at the window display, made a mental note to rearrange some of it, then got in her car to drive quickly through rush-hour Pennington. She eyed the clock, calculating another five minutes to the supermarket, a ten-minute dash round the store to do her shopping, five minutes for parking, another five to get back—suddenly she gasped and jammed on her brakes hard as the back of the car in front loomed close. She wasn't quick enough. There was a grinding impact and she was flung back and then forwards, held by the seatbelt. To an accompaniment of irate tooting of horns a man leapt out of the car in front to inspect the damage, ignoring the traffic damming up behind them.

Groaning in horror, Lowri fought to release the seatbelt, then got out to discover she'd driven into the back of a large, very expensive-looking car. The man bending over to inspect his property straightened and turned to confront her, his face grim with anger but so unmistakable under the street-light that the blood rushed to her face, then receded so suddenly that she felt sick as she sagged against her car in shock.

'What the devil were you playing at?' he demanded, incensed. 'Didn't you see the bloody lights change?' He stopped short as he reached her, his eyes narrowing in abrupt incredulity. He stared at her for a moment then shook his head in disbelief. 'Good lord, *you*, Lowri? I don't believe it. Lowri Morgan, as I live and breathe!'

Before she could find a word to say two policemen arrived on the scene, one of them directing the traffic, the other questioning Adam Hawkridge about the mishap.

'Just one of those things, Officer,' said Adam quickly. 'The lady and I were together. She was following me and I stopped too quickly. My fault entirely.'

On inspection Adam pronounced his car virtually unscathed, unlike Lowri's modest little runabout, which was very much the worse for wear.

'I'll ring my garage,' she said quickly. 'They'll tow it away.'

'Can we leave it here, Officer?' enquired Adam. 'I'll give the lady a lift.'

Minutes later, with the help of the police Lowri's car had been pushed down a side street ready for collection, she'd rung her garage on Adam Hawkridge's car phone and she was sitting in the passenger seat of his Daimler, making a belated effort at apology to a companion whose aura of hostility was almost tangible now they were alone.

'I'm very sorry,' she said as he drove away. 'I was in a panic to get to the shops. I just didn't stop in time.'

'I can't say I'm altogether sorry myself,' he said coldly. 'I always hoped I'd bump into you again one day— though not quite so literally, it's true.'

'I'll give you the name of my insurance company——'

'Unnecessary. I shan't hound you for the sake of a scraped bumper and a new rear light.'

'Thank you. That's very good of you.'

'Good?' he retorted savagely. 'I think I'm being bloody magnanimous for a jilted bridegroom, if that's what you mean.'

'I don't,' she flung back, her penitence vanished. 'I meant that I'm to blame for the accident just now.'

'From my point of view you're culpable for a damn sight more than that!'

Lowri'd had enough. She gestured towards a row of parking spaces at the end of the gardens lining the main street. 'Stop here please. I'll walk the rest of the way.'

'If you've got some idea of disappearing again, forget it,' he said forcibly. 'I'll come with you, then drive you home. I'm not letting you out of my sight until I know where you live.'

Lowri breathed in deeply, struggling for calm. 'I'd much rather you didn't do that.'

He gave her a cold, encompassing glance. 'I take it there's someone who'd object if you came home with a strange man in tow.'

'Yes, there is,' she assured him. 'You can drop me here. Thank you for the lift. My apologies again for running into you.'

'I'll park here for a moment, but you're not going anywhere yet.' A long, sinewy hand grasped her wrist. She eyed it, then looked up at him with hauteur, stiffening as Adam's teeth showed in a brief, frightening smile.

'Not so fast,' he said softly. 'I'm entitled to some explanations. You did quite a lot of damage to my life, Lowri Morgan. It's time you repaired some of it.'

Her mouth tightened. 'The main damage was to your ego, Adam, and since that's obviously alive and well I feel no obligation to give you any explanation at all.'

He eyed her from head to foot without haste. 'You've changed, Lowri.'

'You mean I've grown up,' she retorted. 'I'm not the vulnerable, stupid little girl you once knew, Adam Hawkridge. It may be less than two years in actual time since we last met, but in other ways it feels like a lifetime.'

They stared at each other in open antagonism, each one taking stock of the changes wrought in the other since their last meeting.

During the halcyon days of their relationship Adam had looked younger than his age. Now he appeared more than the mere thirty-four Lowri knew him to be. Responsibility and leadership had etched lines on the familiar, striking face. There was a vertical crease between the heavy straight brows, strands of grey among the brown of his hair, but his eyes were as bright and searching—and cold—as ever.

They took their time in moving over her from the glossy black hair, long now and tied back with a yellow scarf, to her face, which she knew was thinner, its contours emphasised skilfully with make up she hadn't bothered with much in the old days. Adam's eyes moved lower, over her suede bomber jacket and brown wool trousers tucked into fawn suede boots, and she moved restively under the hard, dissecting scrutiny. At last he released her hand, and Lowri stiffened as she caught sight of the dashboard clock.

'I must get back this minute,' she said urgently. 'I'll leave the shopping. Could you please drive me back to— to the place where I work? I've got a colleague waiting for me before she can go.'

'If you insist.'

It was only a short distance to the elegant little side street of shops, most of them converted from houses built when the town had been a fashionable spa in Regency days. Lowri directed Adam past the antique dealer and the jeweller and the shop selling expensive shoes and leather goods, and asked him to pull up outside a double-fronted shop where one window held cleverly arranged baby clothes, the other a beautiful antique cradle, overflowing with lace and ribbons.

'Little Darlings,' said Adam, eyeing the name above the shop. 'Is this where you work?'

'That's right.' Lowri unfastened the seatbelt swiftly and gave him a polite smile. 'Thanks for the lift, Adam. Must dash. I'm sorry we had to meet again in such unfortunate circumstances——'

'Don't think you're getting off as easily as that,' he broke in. 'We need to talk. I'm at the Chesterton, where I'll expect you at eight for dinner.'

'Out of the question!'

He shrugged. 'If you don't, I'll come round here tomorrow—and stay until you consent to a meeting.'

Lowri stared at him, biting her lip.

Adam smiled coolly. 'Tell your husband, or lover, or whatever, that I'm an old friend who simply wants an hour or so of your time, nothing more. Which is the truth, lord knows.'

Lowri caught sight of Jenny peering through the blinds on the door and capitulated suddenly. 'Oh, very well. But I'll be late.'

'No problem. I can wait,' he promised her, in a tone so obviously a threat it raised the hairs on her spine. Lowri dived out of the car and across the broad pavement, shivering as the shop door opened at her approach. She slid inside and banged it shut behind her, ramming the bolts home, then held out her arms for the little girl in Jenny's arms.

'Sorry I was so long, Jenny. Hello, my lovely. Have you been good?'

Rhosyn Morgan beamed, displaying all six teeth as she said 'Mum-mum,' and struggled to get down. Lowri set her down in a playpen filled with toys, as she related her adventure to Jenny, who was the Montessori-trained assistant in charge of the crèche in the basement.

'Gosh, Lowri, what rotten luck,' said Jenny with sympathy as she shrugged into her coat. 'Rosie's been perfectly happy, only she's getting hungry. Where's your shopping, by the way?'

'Never managed it, one way and another.' Lowri blew out her cheeks. 'Never mind, Rosie can have something out of a jar tonight.'

'What about you?'

'I've got to go out, worse luck, if I can sort out a babysitter—anyone free on our list?'

'I'll do it,' offered Jenny. 'I've got nothing on to-night. I might as well look at your telly as mine.'

Thanking her warmly, Lowri locked the door behind Jenny, then picked up her daughter and let her crawl upstairs to the flat on the upper floor of the building. Once there they had a romp together, then Rosie ate her supper with gusto, had a walk round the sitting-room, pulling herself along from chair to chair. Lowri sat on the edge of the sofa, watching her little daughter's every move, raging against the fate which had sent Adam Hawkridge into her life again. The thought of the coming encounter scared her rigid. Yet if she didn't turn up he'd probably carry out his threat and come to the shop next day—the very last thing she wanted.

Rhosyn was hers, Lowri thought fiercely. Adam must never know the false alarm had been a lie. She didn't want his intrusion into the new life she'd made for herself. Bringing up a child single-handed was no bed of roses, but with help from her family she'd managed to achieve control of life both as a mother and as co-owner of the shop downstairs. She had no intention of letting Adam Hawkridge upset her hard-won little apple-cart.

Rosie launched herself away from the nearest chair and toddled across the room to Lowri, holding up her arms in confident appeal.

Lowri swept her up, hugging the little body as she gave her daughter a smacking kiss and took her off to a protracted playtime in the bath. After much splashing and delighted squealing, there were the usual roars of protest as Rosie was taken out and dried, and her dimpled, flailing limbs fastened into her sleeping suit. Then there was a hush as Lowri fed her daughter her bedtime bottle of milk, both of them cuddled close together to enjoy the part of the day Lowri treasured, when work was over and she was alone with her daughter as Rhosyn grew sleepy, and her little body heavy. Lowri put the empty bottle down and held her daughter close. Mine, she thought. All mine.

Lowri hung over the angelic sleeping face once Rhosyn was in her cot, riven by an insecurity which kept her there for longer than usual before she could tear herself away to make reluctant preparations for the evening. Pride, if nothing else, prompted care with her appearance, and when Jenny came back Lowri's hair was coiled up smoothly on top of her head, and she was ready in the raspberry-red dress recently acquired as a reward for her low-calorie diet and the merciless exercises she'd sweated over every night to get her figure back.

Her ears glowing with Jenny's morale-boosting compliments Lowri took a last look at her sleeping daughter, made sure Jenny knew where she was going, then went out into the December night to walk the short distance to the Chesterton, a hotel so far above her touch she'd never yet set foot in it. As she walked briskly she worried over what had brought Adam to the town in the first place, and prayed his stay was just overnight. The thought of him in the vicinity for several days gave her silent hysterics. As she passed through the pillared portico of the hotel Lowri pulled herself together. Now she was here she might as well enjoy the meal. Tonight, she promised herself, the diet could go hang. Her blood-sugars had taken a nose dive at the sight of Adam Hawkridge earlier on. She badly needed some sinful calories to make the evening easier to bear.

Adam was waiting for her in the hotel foyer, reading an evening paper in one of the comfortable leather chairs near the entrance. He sprang to his feet at the sight of her, and seeing him with suddenly objective eyes Lowri felt a pang of unwanted reaction to his physical presence. She stifled it at birth. All that, she reminded herself brusquely, was behind her. This evening was just a chore to be got through. The Adam she'd known no longer existed. The mature, arrogant man smiling at her was no longer a lover. He was a threat.

'Hello, Lowri.' He took her hand for a moment, his eyes gleaming as she withdrew it quickly. 'You look good—roses in your cheeks from the cold.'

'I only hope my nose doesn't try to compete,' she returned lightly. 'It's very warm in here.'

Adam relieved her of her navy overcoat and handed it to a passing waiter. 'Let's have a drink in the bar while we decide what to eat.'

The bar was a small, dimly lit place designed to foster an intimacy which made Lowri uneasy. To her regret most of its customers were quiet twosomes engrossed in each other. She would have preferred noise and laughter, some cheerful background music to alleviate the awkwardness of the situation, and for once would have liked a drink to calm jangled nerves. But in a conscious effort to keep her wits about her Lowri refused anything stronger than a glass of mineral water, ignoring her companion's raised eyebrows.

'Right. Fire away,' said Adam, once their drinks had arrived. 'Why Pennington?'

Lowri settled back in her chair, glad to be spared any preliminary skirmish. 'I've got relatives only a few miles

from here. That's where I went when I left London. I
liked the area, so I stayed on after...' She stopped, biting
her lip.

'After what?' he pounced.

'After I recovered from breaking up with you,' said
Lowri woodenly.

Adam drank some of his Scotch. 'Did that take long?'

'No,' she lied without hesitation.

There was a silence broken by the welcome appearance of a waiter with two enormous menus. By the
time they'd studied the dishes on offer the atmosphere
was less hostile.

'So now you sell baby clothes,' Adam commented,
and smiled quizzically. 'Rather a contrast to sexy
underwear.'

'Ah, but Little Darlings is a bit different from the usual
run of baby shops.'

'In what way?' asked Adam, his business brain quickly
interested.

'We sell nearly new baby clothes,' she explained, glad
of a safer topic. 'People bring us their outgrown children's clothes—in good condition, of course, with a lot
of designer things like Baby Dior, plus cast-off buggies,
prams, furniture and so on. We sell everything at
knockdown prices and take half for ourselves.'

'Surely you don't make much money at that?' asked
Adam, frowning.

'The shop does surprisingly well, but we do offer other
services, too. There's a créche in the basement where
mothers can leave their children with trained staff for
so much an hour. We stock new shoes with a proper
fitting service, keep a list of vetted, approved baby-sit-
ters——' She stopped, flushing. 'I tend to rattle on a bit
about it, I'm afraid.'

'Nice to see such enthusiasm for your work.' Adam
rose to his feet as the waiter came to say their meal was
ready. 'Let's eat. Afterwards, be warned. I intend to learn

everything that's happened to you from the day you left me at the altar—so to speak—right up to the moment when fate sent you crashing into me tonight.'

Lowri's appetite died a sudden death. Her salmon with avocado sauce could have been dust and ashes for all the pleasure she took in the meal. Such a pity, she thought with regret. Meals like this weren't part of her life these days. In fact, she realised suddenly, the last time she'd eaten in such an expensive restaurant had been with the same man who was eyeing her barely touched plate with disapproval.

'That's an odd look on your face,' commented Adam. 'You don't like the food?'

'I don't seem to be very hungry,' she confessed.

'Leave it then and have some pudding. You used to like sweet things. Can't I tempt you?' He smiled, the gleam in his eyes all too familiar.

'No, thank you.' She smiled cheerfully. 'Some coffee would be nice, but nothing else.'

'Then let's go back to the bar to drink it.'

The bar was crowded by this time. But like magic, as always happened for Adam, some people got up to leave as they arrived, and he swiftly installed her in the vacated corner and suggested brandy, or a liqueur.

'No, really.' She shook her head. 'My day starts early. I daren't risk a hangover.'

'I don't think half a glass of wine can have done you much harm.'

'Exactly. That was my intention.'

Lowri poured coffee, and without thinking added one sugar lump to Adam's cup and passed it to him, then could have kicked herself at the smug look on his face.

'Your memory's good, Lowri.'

'Only for trivia.' She smiled sweetly.

'Like promises of marriage?' His eyes bored into hers, all trace of warmth vanished.

Lowri shrugged, oddly calm now the gloves were off. 'I never actually promised to marry you, Adam. You just took my acquiescence for granted.'

His eyes narrowed ominously. 'You mean that you never had the least intention of turning up that day?'

'That's right.' She drained her cup, then refilled it, gesturing politely at his. 'More?'

'No. I need some cognac.' Adam signalled to the waiter, then turned back to Lowri. 'Why?'

'Why what?'

'You know damn well,' he snapped, his wide mouth tightening. 'Why did you string me along like that? What had I done? I asked you to marry me, remember.'

'True. But with such undisguised reluctance that I felt like some tawdry little schemer who'd set out to trap you into it.' Lowri shrugged. 'I was all too obviously some encumbrance you couldn't shake off. Whereas to me you were the only man I'd ever fallen in love with—up to then, at least.'

Adam paused to allow the waiter to serve him the brandy, then drank half of it in one swallow and set down the glass to stab Lowri with a cold, accusing look. 'I rang Rupert that day, afraid you'd had an accident when you didn't turn up. I couldn't take it in at first when he said you'd gone away. Then when I went round to collect the letter my reception from Sarah froze the blood in my veins.' He smiled grimly. 'I've not set eyes on either of them since. They made it bloody plain I was *persona non grata* in their home. I find it hard to forgive you that. I like them both. I was very fond of young Dominic and Emily too, but I doubt Sarah will ever let me near them again.'

Lowri shrugged. 'Sarah's family, remember. The Morgans tend to be a clannish tribe.'

Adam stared at her. 'Talking of which, no doubt you heard about my abortive trip to Wales to look for you?'

'Oh, yes. My father rang me the moment you left.'

'My reception was a damn sight worse there.'

'What did you expect?'

'Hell, Lowri, I was trying to find out where you'd gone. At the time my life was so fraught, one way and another, the last thing I needed was a chase about the countryside looking for you.'

'I didn't ask you to look for me,' she pointed out, unmoved. 'And one trip to Cwmderwen hardly counts as chasing about the countryside.'

Adam controlled himself with effort. 'It was a sheer waste of time, anyway. Your father flatly refused to tell me where you were, and all but threw me out. I never even met your stepmother. There wasn't a damned thing I could do, so I went back to London and did my best to forget you'd ever existed.'

'Very sensible.'

He eyed her morosely. 'You obviously forgot me easily enough if you're with someone else these days.'

'I'm sure you did the same.'

There was a pause while Adam finished his brandy.

'Strangely enough I didn't,' he said expressionlessly. 'No time for women these days. Work fills my life.'

Lowri gave him a sceptical smile. 'That's hard to believe.'

'The truth often is.' His answering smile lacked mirth. 'My mother's quite worried. At one time she complained about my endless string of girlfriends—her words, not mine. Now she complains because there aren't any at all.'

'None?'

'Not even one. She keeps telling me I need to settle down and produce a family.' His mouth twisted. 'Fortunately she'll never know how near I once came to granting her wish.'

Lowri gathered up her bag and scarf. 'Right. Well now you've discovered what you wanted to know——'

'Not so fast.' Adam's hand shot across the table to stay her. 'I don't know anything like enough, Lowri. I want to know where you went, why you wouldn't let anyone tell me where you were.'

'I told you where, Adam. I went to stay with relatives and swore everyone to secrecy because I didn't want to see you again. Simple, really.' She got up, a determined set to her mouth. 'Now I must go.'

Adam jumped to his feet. 'I'd drive you home, but the brandy was one drink too many. If you'll wait here for a moment I'll get someone to call you a cab.'

Lowri opened her mouth to say it was only a short walk to the flat then changed her mind. If she did that Adam would promptly volunteer to walk with her.

As they waited in the foyer Lowri searched for something neutral to say to ease the tension between them.

'Thank you for a delicious meal,' she came up with finally.

Adam eyed her sardonically. 'You ate very little of it.'

Another pause.

'Are you travelling back tomorrow?' she asked politely, wishing the taxi would turn up.

'I'm not sure yet.' He shrugged. 'It depends on the success of my mission.'

To Lowri's relief her ordeal ended with the arrival of the taxi, and with a bright smile she held out her hand to Adam.

'Goodbye, then. My apologies again about the car.'

'A small price to pay for the privilege of meeting you again.' Adam's smile mocked her as instead of shaking her hand he raised it to his lips then to her surprise let her go, making no move to follow her as she walked out of the hotel. Lowri's eyebrows rose. She'd fully expected Adam to see her into the taxi, if only to learn where she lived.

After an evening of unrelenting strain followed by a restless night Lowri was desperately tired next morning when the usual imperious demand came through the intercom to wake her up. But in an instant she was out of bed, yawning, and into her dressing-gown to collect her daughter, who was standing up in the cot in her little room, banging the rails with her rattle.

'Ba-ba, ba-ba,' Rhosyn chanted, then dropped the rattle to stretch out her hand to Lowri. 'Mum-mum!' She greeted her mother with her irresistible toothy grin, and Lowri picked her up and gave her a smacking kiss, then began changing her into the clothes put ready the night before. When her daughter was arrayed in a red sweater and tights, denim dungarees printed with huge red and yellow dots, the tiny feet in red checked sneakers, Lowri took Rhosyn through to the kitchen, installed her in her high chair and put a bottle of formula in the bottle warmer and filled the kettle. She made tea and toast, tied a bib round the little neck, put cereal in a bowl, added milk from the bottle to it, then sat down to feed her child, thankful the routine was so automatic after her wakeful night. Rhosyn ate her cereal hungrily, drank the rest of the milk in the bottle, then munched some toast soldiers while Lowri ate her own meagre breakfast.

Afterwards she set Rhosyn on the floor in the sitting-room with her sack of toys, made sure all the child locks were on the cupboards and the safety covers on the electricity sockets, put the gate in place in the open doorway between the two rooms and tidied the kitchen hurriedly. She put some laundry in the washing machine, sterilised Rhosyn's bottles and washed the dishes, one eye in constant surveillance on her daughter as the busy little girl took toys from the sack, toddled across the room with them to pile them against the gate, then trotted back again to fetch more.

Later Lowri took the child into the bedroom while she dressed and got ready for her day in the shop below. Rhosyn took the pile of magazines from the bedside table, as she always did, and sat on the floor looking at them, tearing the odd page as she tried to open them, while Lowri pulled on black jersey trousers and turtle-necked sweater and added a yellow corduroy overshirt cinched in at the waist with a wide black belt. She tied back her hair with a yellow scarf, made up her face with the swift efficiency she'd learned in the past few months, then changed Rhosyn's nappy again. Afterwards Lowri took her back to the sitting-room and spent some time reading and playing with her, and, in the end, sat cuddling the child in her arms on the sofa while the little girl slept for the half-hour nap she consented to at this hour.

When Lowri arrived in the shop at ten, as usual, her partner, Fran Hobbs, had opened up, Jenny was in the basement crèche ready to receive Rhosyn and any other comers, and several Christmas shoppers were already bargain-hunting among the clothes and furniture. Little Darlings was in business.

By five-thirty that evening Lowri was ready to drop. Because Fran opened up and did the first hour in the morning she left early, leaving Lowri and Jenny to cope for the last hour of the day. With Christmas only two weeks away the shop had been gratifyingly busy, but after hours of helping mothers with their choices, fitting toddlers with shoes and helping Jenny out now and again down in the crèche with only a short break upstairs for Rhosyn's lunch and rest, Lowri felt tired. At this stage she always brought Rhosyn up to play in one of the playpens set out under a battery of mobiles hanging from the ceiling, and tonight her little daughter lay happily on her back, cuddling her fluffy rabbit and waving at the moving ducks and clowns and Disney characters suspended above her while Lowri and Jenny did some tidying up preparatory to shutting up shop.

'That's about it, I think,' yawned Jenny. 'Everything's shipshape down below. Shall I lock up?'

'Yes, please!' said Lowri fervently. 'My feet are killing me——' She groaned inwardly as the bell went to admit a last-minute shopper, managed a smile, then stood very still, suddenly tense as a tigress with her cub. Her customer was Adam Hawkridge, tall and formidable in a dark city greatcoat, with flakes of snow melting in his thick brown hair.

CHAPTER NINE

'GOOD evening, sir,' said Jenny politely. 'How can I help you?'

He gave her a smile. 'I'm afraid I'm not a customer. I've come to see Miss Morgan.'

Jenny shot Lowri a questioning glance.

'It's all right.' Lowri nodded reassuringly. 'You go off. I'll lock up behind you and let Mr Hawkridge out later.' She turned politely to Adam. 'I imagine you've come to discuss the accident yesterday. Was the damage to your car worse than you thought?'

Behind his back Jenny, enlightened, pulled a sympathetic face, collected her coat then said goodnight and went out into the snowy December night, leaving an atmosphere hardly less arctic behind her.

Praying Rhosyn would stay quiet, Lowri thrust a strand of hair behind her ear and looked up at Adam in cold enquiry. 'I thought you'd have left by now. Was your mission unsuccessful after all?'

'The business part was very satisfactory,' he assured her, looking round the shop with interest. 'On the personal side I need to put some work in. You left a lot of questions unanswered last night, Lowri, so before I leave tomorrow I thought I'd call round and have a little chat.' Suddenly his eyes narrowed as he caught sight of the sleeping child. 'Good lord—has one of your customers left her baby behind?'

'No,' said Lowri, resigned. 'If you must know, she's mine.'

Adam gazed down at the child, stunned, then back at Lowri. '*Yours*? What's her name?'

118

'Rhosyn.'

'Unusual.'

'Welsh for rose. I'm afraid she gets Rosie from most people.'

'Including her father?'

Lowri stared at him impassively, saying nothing.

Adam returned to contemplation of the child, who looked very small and defenceless clutching a pink bunny almost as big as herself. Feathery strands of hair curled on the still visible crown of her head, one shoe had been kicked off, exposing a minute red foot. And suddenly, as though aware of his scrutiny, Rhosyn opened big dark eyes like her mother's and gave him a sleepy smile.

'Hello,' he said softly, and smiled back. He stared down at the child, fascinated, making Lowri very uneasy. 'She's the image of you.'

'So I'm told,' she said shortly.

'How old is she?'

'Nine months.'

Adam shot a hostile look at her. 'You got to know her father pretty bloody quickly!'

'Yes.' Lowri smiled sweetly. 'Love at first sight.' Noting signs of restlessness from her daughter, she bent quickly to pick her up. 'I'm afraid it's bathtime. I'll have to ask you to go now.'

'I was hoping for an introduction to the man in your life,' said Adam, his eyes bright with challenge. 'Tact forbade me to ask about his reaction to your night out with me, by the way. I take it you're not actually married to him?'

'No.'

'You're still allergic to marriage, then!'

'Not at all,' she returned. 'I'll get round to it one day, no doubt. But if I don't it's not really any business of yours, Adam.'

'It was once,' he reminded her cuttingly.

'All that seems a long time ago.' Lowri struggled with her fidgeting daughter, who was demanding to get down. 'Look, I've got to take her upstairs.'

'Her father's not home yet?'

'That's right, he's not.' Lowri smiled politely. 'Goodnight, Adam.'

Adam's lips tightened. 'All right, Lowri, you win. Or rather this young lady does. Goodnight.' He put out a finger and touched Rhosyn's flushed cheek. 'Bye.'

'Bye-bye,' said Rhosyn and flapped her hand at him, beaming.

Lowri held her breath as Adam stared at the child in amazement.

'My word, young lady, you're pretty forward for your age!' He looked at Lowri quizzically. 'Do babies usually talk at nine months?'

'She doesn't talk, she just says "Mum-mum" and "bye-bye",' said Lowri, then wished she hadn't as Adam raised a sardonic eyebrow.

'I thought the first word was usually "Daddy",' he drawled, and went to the door. 'I may call in again before I leave,' he added, and gave her a deeply disturbing smile before he went out into the snowy night.

Lowri dumped Rhosyn into the playpen and hurried to lock up. Once the shop was dark apart from the lights trained on the window arrangements she scooped up her daughter and hurried up the stairs to the safety of the flat, feeling as if she'd escaped danger by the skin of her teeth.

A couple of action-packed hours later, when Rhosyn was finally asleep, Lowri made herself one of the low-calorie rice dishes on her diet. She sat down on the sofa with a book and a cup of coffee to eat it, still desperately worried about Adam. Which was silly, she informed herself trenchantly. Even if Adam did learn the truth about Rhosyn it wouldn't matter. The baby was hers, and hers alone. He'd forfeited all right to Rhosyn the day he'd accused her mother of getting pregnant to blackmail him into marriage.

Lowri had just emerged from the bath, her wet hair swathed in a towel, when the doorbell rang. She lifted the receiver cautiously.

'Yes?'

'It's Adam. Let me in, Lowri.'

'Certainly not.' She slammed down the instrument, but Adam replaced his finger on the buzzer and kept it there until she answered it.

'Go away,' she said furiously.

'Not until I've seen you.'

'It's not convenient—I'm not alone.'

'The only one up there with you is Rhosyn. So let me in, Lowri.'

She hesitated, in an agony of indecision.

'I won't go away,' said Adam, with a finality which won him the day.

'Oh very well,' she said angrily. 'But only for a minute or two. I'm tired.'

She released the catch on the outer door, then raced to check on Rhosyn. She turned the baby on her side and covered her up securely, then braced herself and went to open the door to Adam's knock.

He stood outside on the landing, dressed in the same dark overcoat, a smile playing at the corners of his mouth as he eyed her towel-swathed head and all-enveloping scarlet wool dressing-gown.

Lowri went ahead of him into the sitting-room. 'Come in here, please.'

Adam followed her into the small room, looking round him at the functional furniture and unornamented walls, the only splash of colour the crimson silk curtains, which added a touch of luxury to an otherwise stringently practical décor.

'So this is where you live,' he commented. 'May I take off my coat?'

'Are you staying long enough to make that necessary? I'm expecting my—my boyfriend back soon.'

Adam shook his head decisively. 'I don't believe you. After I left you tonight I made some enquiries. You live alone, Lowri. Except for the baby.'

Lowri stared at him malevolently, then shrugged. 'I see. In that case you'd better sit down and wait for a moment. My hair's dripping down my neck. I need to dry it a little. There's an evening paper somewhere.'

She hurried to her bedroom, her mind in a ferment as she rubbed furiously at her hair, then brushed it back from her face and secured it with a ribbon, hoping she wouldn't catch pneumonia by leaving it so wet. She eyed the dressing gown for a moment, then shrugged. That could stay. If Adam got a glimpse of striped pyjama it served him right for barging his way in like this.

Adam got up from the sofa when she rejoined him, a strangely bleak look on his face. 'Why did you pretend someone shared this place with you, Lowri?'

'I didn't. You asked me if anyone would object if I brought a strange man home and I said yes,' she said coldly. 'Rhosyn likes all my attention, I'm afraid.'

'So where's Rhosyn's father?'

'He and I are no longer in a relationship.' Lowri forced a smile. 'I'm afraid I don't keep anything to drink in the flat—alcoholic, I mean. Would you like some coffee?'

'No, I would not! Thanks,' he added belatedly. He leaned back on the sofa, eyeing her narrowly as she sat down in a nearby armchair. 'I went round to the garage this evening.'

'Garage?'

'The one who towed away your car. They said it would be ready next week.' Adam raised a sardonic eyebrow. 'The owner's a friendly sort of chap. Said he'd do his best for you. Promised he wouldn't do you over unnecessary parts, and so on, just because you're a woman on your own.'

Lowri stared at him, incensed. 'I never realised Mr Booker was such a chauvinist.'

'He told me you're a very plucky little thing, single parent and so on and making such a success of the business. He told me you lived over the shop, too.' Adam's smile was wry. 'You didn't tell me you owned it.'

'I don't. I'm in partnership with someone else. Fran lives with her husband and family not far from here.'

'I didn't realise you were a lady of substance.'

'I came into a very modest sum of money on my twenty-first birthday. My mother left it in trust for me.' Lowri smiled coldly. 'It came in very handy, one way and another.'

Adam's answering smile was ominous. 'This chap Booker said something else very interesting, by the way.'

'Oh?'

'Apparently you had the car serviced recently—wanted it in good time for your daughter's birthday. Which,' he added very deliberately, 'he told me was last week. Rhosyn's older than you made out.'

Lowri sat very still, her eyes on his.

'You lied to me,' he said harshly. 'Not once but twice. Rhosyn is not nine months old, neither was she a false alarm. She's mine! Why the hell did you lie to me? Why didn't you go through with the marriage, you——?'

'Stupid woman?' she finished for him. Her chin lifted. 'Let's get something straight, Adam. The accident of conception does not make Rhosyn yours in any way other than purely biological. You didn't want her, so she's mine—mine alone. And I didn't marry you because I couldn't face the thought of life with a man who was taking me on sufferance. It would be nice to say I stopped caring for you the moment you accused me of engineering the whole situation—but I didn't, more fool me.

I hoped right up to the last minute that you'd come round, revert to the lover I'd once had. When it was obvious that wasn't going to happen I made other plans. If it soothes your ego a little I freely admit I was in love with you, Adam. Otherwise I couldn't have let you make love to me. But to you I was just a surprisingly sexy little playmate to take to bed. You cooled off so completely once you knew I was pregnant that it painted a very vivid picture of what our life together would be. I couldn't bear the thought of it. So I lied. And I've never regretted it,' she added, then smiled sardonically. 'It was hard work keeping my father—not to mention Rupert— from telling you the truth. But in the end I had my own way.'

'No wonder your father threw me out of his house,' said Adam bitterly. 'Surely you told him I was willing to marry you?'

Lowri glared at him. '*Willing*? How very good of you, to be sure! But I needed someone passionately eager to marry me, not just willing.'

Suddenly a wail through the intercom put an end to the argument. Lowri leapt to her feet and ran to find Rhosyn was standing up in her cot, tears streaming down her cheeks. She held up her arms and Lowri scooped her up to hug her close.

'Oh, darling, you're all soggy. Mummy can't have fastened your nappy properly.' Her heart still thumping angrily, Lowri put the baby down on a bathtowel on the floor and changed her swiftly, then handed over Rhosyn's bunny. 'There, *cariad*, cuddle Flopsy while I change your bed.'

But Rhosyn scrambled up, clinging to Lowri's knees, her eyes like saucers as Adam appeared in the doorway.

For a moment all three seemed frozen in tableau, than in a strained, constricted voice he asked, 'Can I help?'

'No!' Lowri sat her daughter down again. 'I'll just change her cot then she can go back to sleep.'

But Rhosyn wasn't having any. She pulled herself to her feet on the end of the cot and stood eyeing Adam with hostile dark eyes. He laughed involuntarily.

'You look just like your mother.' He held out his hand coaxingly. 'Won't you come and talk to me?'

'Leave her alone!' ordered Lowri. 'If she gets excited I'll never get her back to sleep.'

But Rhosyn's curiosity had overcome her caution. Dropping the rabbit she trotted across the room to Adam, who watched her progress with something so like pride that Lowri went cold.

'She can walk!' he exclaimed.

Lowri ignored him as she whipped off damp sheets and replaced them with dry ones, tucking them in with a speed and precision any ward sister would have approved.

'Can I pick her up?' he asked, never taking his eyes off the child.

'She won't let you. She doesn't see many men.' Lowri added a cellular blanket to the bed then turned round to see her daughter in the careful, unpractised embrace of her father, who was holding the child in such a precarious way that Lowri would have laughed if it had been anyone else.

Rhosyn stared curiously at the strange face so close to hers. She reached up a hand to tug on Adam's hair, then turned to look at her mother, as if asking what this strange, male person was doing in her bedroom.

'You can give her to me now,' said Lowri, wanting to tear her child from Adam's arms.

He surrendered the small warm body with a reluctance which struck fear into Lowri's heart. She switched on the bottle-warmer then wrapped the baby in a blanket and went into the kitchen to get a bottle of milk from the fridge, Rhosyn held tightly in her arms.

'Lowri,' said Adam, when she returned. 'Don't look like that. I wouldn't harm a hair of her head. You must know that.'

Lowri put the bottle into the warmer and sat down in a rocking chair with Rhosyn cuddled close. 'If you'll go back into the other room I'll join you as soon as I've put her back to bed.'

'Can't I stay to watch her drink her milk?'

'No.' Lowri refused to look at him. 'She'll never settle if you do.'

Adam left with such obvious reluctance that Lowri had to force herself to relax, deliberately emptying her mind of all the fear and worry crowding it as she fed her child, then cuddled her to sleep. Gently she put Rhosyn in the cot, drew the blankets over her and tiptoed from the room.

Adam was prowling restlessly round the sitting-room when she rejoined him. 'Lowri, I'd appreciate that coffee now.'

'All right,' she said ungraciously. 'But while I'm in the kitchen don't even think of going into Rhosyn's room.'

His face hardened. 'What the hell do you think I'd do if I did?'

'Disturb her—wake her up.' Lowri eyed him levelly. 'My day starts early, Adam. I need my sleep. And I won't get it if Rhosyn decides she needs entertainment at two in the morning.'

His mouth twisted. 'I promise I shan't move from the spot.'

'I'm afraid you'll have to go back to the paper while you wait. I do own a television, but it's in my bedroom.'

'For lack of any other company?' he said swiftly.

'No. Because now Rosie's walking I keep all electrical gadgets well out of her way,' returned Lowri coldly. 'I'll make that coffee.'

When she got back with it, Adam was doing the crossword in the paper. Lowri handed him a mug and resumed her chair to drink her own coffee. 'No biscuits, I'm afraid, I'm on a diet.'

He frowned. 'Why? You're thinner than you used to be.'

'Only because I work at it.'

Adam drank some of his coffee in silence, his eyes brooding, then he set the mug down on the table beside him and leaned forward, looking at her commandingly. 'Lowri, what are we going to do about this?'

Her eyes narrowed. 'About what?'

'About Rhosyn. As you know perfectly well,' he added with barely controlled violence.

'Nothing, Adam.'

'What do you mean, nothing!' His eyes glittered coldly. 'She happens to be my daughter.'

'That's right, Adam,' snapped Lowri. 'You just "happen" to be her father. It was an accident. And you hated the very thought of being tied down with a baby, remember. So I solved the problem for you.'

'You had no right to take it on yourself to do so,' he said savagely.

'I had every right!' She glared at him. 'Rhosyn is mine, Adam. So go away and leave us alone. We don't need you! I won't have you upsetting our lives just because you've discovered some stray paternal fondness you never knew you had.'

'I might have discovered it a bloody sight sooner, given the chance,' he retorted, white with anger. 'It's your fault I don't know my daughter, nor she her father. Left to me, you and I would be married and I'd have been there at her birth——' He stopped suddenly, looking grim. 'Who *was* with you, Lowri?'

She smiled mockingly. 'I was probably the least lonely single parent in the entire world. Sarah and her sisters Rhia and Mari-Sian were actually with me in the room, but my father and Rupert were downstairs with Holly and young Huw Morgan, my new little brother.'

Adam breathed in deeply. 'So the absence of a father went entirely unnoticed—and unlamented.'

'I wasn't in a hospital,' she told him quietly. 'I gave birth to Rhosyn at Rhia's home. She was the relative I went to when I left London. She's Sir Charles Hadley's widow.'

'Hadley Pharmaceuticals?'

'That's the one.'

His mouth twisted. 'I didn't realise you had such influential connections.'

'Kindness, not influence, is the key word in this instance,' Lowri contradicted. 'Rhia has two teenage stepdaughters, but never gave Charles a child of her own, to her great sorrow. The girls were away at boarding school, Rhia was still grieving over Charles's death, so when I told Sarah about my little problem——'

'You swore *me* to secrecy,' he reminded her swiftly, his jaw set.

'She came on me by surprise when I was crying my eyes out a few days before I was supposed to be marrying you.'

'Supposed being the operative word!'

Lowri's eyes flashed dangerously. 'As I said, she found me in tears because I was in the process of facing up to the truth. That you were never going to revert to the lover I'd been so besotted with. Sarah got the truth out of me, and decided Rhia was the answer to my problem.'

'I assumed you'd go home to your father.'

'He wanted me to.' Lowri's mouth twisted. 'A few heated arguments sizzled along the wires between London and Cwmderwen on the subject, believe me. But Dad already had more than enough on his plate with Holly, who was very poorly before Huw's birth and worried everyone to death. Besides Dad's very fond of Rhia, and Mari-Sian, who's frighteningly clever and lectures in modern languages at Cambridge, convinced him that my company, even with all its attendant problems—or maybe because of them—was just the thing her sister needed. So he gave in.'

'Wasn't Lady Hadley afraid your sorry little tale would be a bad example to her stepdaughters?' said Adam cuttingly.

Lowri gave him a hostile glare. 'On the contrary. Rhia felt my predicament served as a graphic warning to them in their future dealings with your sex.'

There was a fraught silence in the room for an interval, while Lowri stared down at her tightly clasped hands, very much aware that Adam never took his eyes off her averted face.

'So,' he said at last, at the point where Lowri thought she'd scream if the silence lasted any longer. 'I'm refused anything to do with my daughter.'

Lowri raised implacable dark eyes to his face. 'That's right, Adam. I like our lives the way they are.'

'What about Rhosyn?' he said swiftly. 'Shouldn't her preferences come into it somewhere?'

'At the moment I am all the preference she possesses. And I intend to keep it that way.' Lowri looked pointedly at her watch.

'I'm not going yet, so you can stop that,' he said angrily.

'You won't change my mind, Adam, however long you stay. So you might as well go.'

He jumped to his feet and stood in front of the fireplace, glaring down at her. 'I'm not the first man to feel shock at being rushed into marriage, dammit! Are you going to make me pay for the rest of my life because I didn't embrace the idea with open arms?'

'You've missed the point,' she said, unmoved. 'I wasn't the one rushing the marriage. You were. And for all the wrong reasons. Saving face, at a guess. The right thing to do and all that—which I could have coped with. Just.

But you accused me of getting pregnant deliberately to trap you into marriage, Adam. And that I just couldn't take.'

'So you agreed to a wedding just so you could punish me by not turning up,' he said heavily.

She nodded. 'More or less. It was deeply satisfying at the time.'

Adam picked up his coat and shrugged into it. 'So we've reached an impasse. You can't forgive me because I said something stupid in the heat of the moment. While I can't forgive you for keeping his only grandchild secret from my father before he died.'

Lowri stared at him, arrested. 'Your father's dead? I didn't know.'

'He knew he had only a short time to live when he agreed to the cruise. At least he hung on long enough to enjoy that. But his condition was the reason for rushing me into taking over the company before he went.'

'Did you know?'

'Yes. And my mother knew too, of course. They never kept secrets from each other.'

The words hung in the air for a moment.

'But they were different,' said Lowri very quietly. 'They loved each other.'

'You said just now that you loved me,' he reminded her.

'Oh, I did, Adam. Past tense,' she added, to remove all possible doubt.

He stared down at her in frustration, anger in every line of him. 'The last word on your part, I assume.'

'Yes.' Lowri went to the door and opened it. 'Goodbye, Adam.'

He gave her a searing look as he went out into the hall. 'I take it there's no possibility of a last look at my daughter?'

'None at all,' she said without emotion.

'You've developed a bloody good talent for cruelty since the old days, Lowri,' he said with bitterness.

She smiled disdainfully. 'It's not really surprising. To quote Henry James, Adam, I was taught by masters. Well, one master really. You.'

CHAPTER TEN

AFTER Adam had gone Lowri shivered with reaction for minutes on end, until at last the need to talk to someone was so overwhelming that she rang Sarah to tell her what had happened.

Sarah whistled after she'd heard Lowri out. 'How did Adam react to your punchline?'

Lowri sighed. 'He stood there like a statue and just looked at me. Then he turned away. Sort of in slow motion. And left without another word.'

Sarah paused. 'Do you still feel bitter towards him?'

'I don't know how I feel. I just wish I hadn't met him again.'

'How was he with Rhosyn?'

'Fascinated. Terrifyingly so.'

'Understandable, in the circumstances.'

'But she's not a son to train up for the business—she's a girl.'

'What difference does that make? Besides, she's not just any little girl, is she! She's his daughter, Lowri.'

'No, she's not, Sal—she's mine!'

'You know what I mean,' said Sarah soothingly. 'He could help, you know, *cariad*. Financially.'

'I don't need help——' Lowri bit her lip. 'Oh Sarah, I'm sorry. I'll always be grateful for the help you've all given me. But Adam's help I'd rather do without.'

The run-up to Christmas was so busy Lowri was thankful she had little time to think. She was due to drive to Cwmderwen once she'd closed the shop on Christmas Eve, and for weeks she'd been looking forward to a break with her father and Holly, and little Huw. The shop looked festive with cut-out figures from nursery rhymes and flights of gilt cherubs, and a Christmas tree in the window in place of the crib. And in the flat upstairs Lowri decorated a tiny tree for Rhosyn, and hung paper-chains and sprigs of holly in the sitting-room. Takings in the shop were good and the crèche was doing a roaring trade while busy mothers did their Christmas shopping. But underneath it all Lowri couldn't rid herself of the unease which hung over her like a cloud since her encounter with Adam.

Her reaction was fierce when she found his visit to her garage had been motivated by more than mere idle curiosity. Adam Hawkridge had not only settled the bill for the quite extensive repairs, but had paid for a set of new tyres for her car.

Lowri's thank-you letter was a chore she laboured over for hours before she was satisfied with the polite, impersonal little note she finally addressed to Hawk Electronics, since she had no idea if Adam still lived in the riverside flat. Her first instinct was to send a cheque to him immediately for the amount, but after giving it thought something stayed her hand. The look in Adam's eyes as he'd left her that night had haunted her ever since. To throw his money back in his face smacked of a cruelty no lesson could ever have taught her.

Three days before Christmas a mammoth present was delivered to the shop for Rhosyn.

'Good heavens,' said Fran Hobbs as a glorious rocking horse emerged from the carton. 'Who in the world sent Rosie that?'

'No card,' said Lowri, pink-cheeked. 'Must be from Rhia. She's spending Christmas in Gstaad with the girls. She obviously thought it would come in handy in the shop, or down in the play area—no room for it up in the flat, that's for sure.'

Next day more packages arrived, but Lowri took these upstairs to open later in private, unwilling to risk any more embarrassment in front of Fran and Jenny. Not that either of them was ever tactless enough to ask about Rhosyn's father—or lack of one.

Later, when Rhosyn was tucked up in her cot, Lowri forced herself to have a bath and eat her supper before she let herself open the parcels. She took the wrappings off slowly at last, then stared as she opened a box full of clothes for her daughter: diminutive dungarees and expensive sweaters, cute little training shoes, a towelling robe and a strawberry-pink ski-jacket. She raised an eyebrow at the designer labels, then took out the card which lay at the bottom of the box.

'To Rhosyn,' it said, in familiar bold handwriting, 'with love'.

Again Lowri wanted to stuff everything back in the box and send it straight to Hawk Electronics. But after a moment she calmed down, trying to be fair. There'd been no veto on presents. And Rhosyn was too young to know where the clothes came from. Lowri shrugged, hardening herself to a practical point of view. After Rosie'd grown out of them they'd fetch a good price down in the shop. The larger of the other two parcels contained a long-haired teddy-bear as big as Rhosyn, but the smaller one was addressed to Lowri. She eyed it malevolently, wondering if Adam had the gall to think he could win her round with presents.

When she removed the paper Lowri found a small jeweller's box. Her eyes narrowed dangerously, then opened wide when she discovered a small gold cricket bat with a tiny gold cricket ball attached to it. Adam Hawkridge was too clever by half, she thought mutinously, staring at the brooch through a veil of sudden, treacherous tears. Nostalgia was a sneaky, underhand way to undermine her defences.

Next day was sheer chaos in the shop. Jenny needed to get off early in the afternoon and had asked permission to bring in her young sister Kay, who was on Christmas leave from her nanny-training. The extra pair of hands in the crèche came in useful, especially when Lowri needed to take Rhosyn upstairs for her lunch and a short nap. But with Jenny off in the afternoon it was hectic, and Fran volunteered to stay until closing time. At one stage Lowri dashed out to buy more of the balloons they were handing out to all their little clients over the Christmas period, then when the final wave of mothers rushed in to collect their children she went down to the basement to give Kay a hand.

'Where's Rhosyn?' she said to the girl in an undertone as Kay zipped up a little boy's windcheater.

Kay looked blank. 'What do you mean, Miss Morgan? Haven't you got her?'

Lowri felt the blood drain away from her face. 'No!' she said, and raced up the stairs while Kay handed the child over to his mother.

'Have you seen Rhosyn?' panted Lowri, grabbing Fran.

'Dear heaven, no. Isn't she down——?' Fran shook her head. 'Obviously not or you wouldn't be asking me.' She turned on Kay, who'd come running upstairs, white-faced as Lowri. 'Now then, young lady. What's all this?'

Kay began to sob. 'A lady—came down—and said she was Rhosyn's grandmother, that Rosie's mummy wanted her upstairs. I didn't know—I thought——'

Lowri pulled herself together, forcing herself to be gentle. 'All right, Kay—calm down. Can you describe the woman?'

For a while Kay was too hysterical to say a word, but eventually a sharp admonition from Fran dried her up sufficiently to try to remember. 'Grey hair—elderly—nice clothes.'

'How did she talk—any accent?' said Lowri, trying not to panic.

'Sort of posh—you know.' Kay stared at her in misery. 'Oh, Miss Morgan, I could kill myself. But she was so nice!'

'Nice women don't steal babies,' said Fran forcefully, and went to the telephone. 'I'm calling the police.'

'Hang on a minute,' said Lowri in a strange voice. 'You two get off home. I'd better do some checking before I involve the police.'

'You mean you know who might have taken her?'

'No. But I've suddenly got a very strong suspicion.'

Fran's eyebrows rose. 'Do I take it the description actually fits Rhosyn's grandmother?'

'I don't know. I've never met her.' Lowri breathed in deeply. 'Look, I can't explain now—your family will be waiting for you, Fran. If I need you I'll ring you.'

'You're taking this much too calmly, love——'

'Then I must be a bloody good actress!' said Lowri with sudden savagery, and Fran nodded briskly in comprehension, hugged her hard and shooed the distraught teenager out of the shop. 'Right. I'll see Kay home, feed my lot and come back later. Sooner if you need me,' she added as she closed the door.

Lowri flew upstairs, in case by some strange quirk of fate her adventurous baby had somehow made it up to the flat on her own. But the rooms were empty. As she'd known they'd be. She picked up the phone, her breath rasping in her chest as she punched the buttons for the number of Hawk Electronics. She was put through to Adam's assistant. He informed her that Mr Hawkridge had just left and he himself was not at liberty to divulge his employer's home telephone number. In an agony of frustration Lowri tried the number of the Wapping flat and got Adam's terse voice on his answering machine. At screaming point, she left a brief, urgent message for him to ring her immediately he got in, then rang

Directory Enquiries and asked for the number of the family home in Sussex.

In her anguish Lowri punched out the third number twice before she got it right, then sagged against the wall as a friendly voice gave the number and then said,

'Alice Hawkridge speaking.'

For a moment Lowri couldn't say a word and the woman said 'Hello? Is someone there? Hello?'

'Mrs Hawkridge,' said Lowri hoarsely. 'You won't know me——'

'Who is this?'

'My name's Lowri Morgan——'

'Lowri? Oh my dear, how wonderful to hear from you. Adam wouldn't let me contact you but I did so hope— what is it? What's the matter?' asked Mrs Hawkridge sharply, as Lowri gave a groan like someone in mortal agony.

'My *baby*,' she got out. 'Someone's stolen Rhosyn.' She sobbed her story out, even admitting she'd suspected Mrs Hawkridge of taking Rhosyn away.

There was a gasp of horror down the line, then a resolute, 'And why shouldn't you? You don't know me, after all. But I didn't,' added Mrs Hawkridge unsteadily.

'I know, I know, I only wish you had!' cried Lowri. 'At least I'd know where she was.'

'My dear, ring the police. Adam's on his way to supper with me at this very moment. I'll contact him on his car phone. You ring the police now!'

The police were wonderfully prompt. While Lowri was answering Fran's phone call the outer doorbell rang, and within seconds the small sitting-room seemed crowded as a detective inspector, accompanied by his sergeant and a woman police constable arrived to hear the details. Lowri, tear-stained but more composed by this time, answered their questions as fully as she could and supplied them with a description of Rhosyn's clothes, and gave them photographs and every scrap of information she could piece together as relevant.

'Don't worry about relevance, Mrs Morgan,' said Inspector Cox, 'tell us anything at all. We'll decide whether it's important.' He nodded to the woman constable. 'Maggie will make you some coffee.'

'Thank you.' Lowri took a deep, unsteady breath. 'But first of all I'm not Mrs Morgan, I'm Miss.'

'I see. Does that mean you live here alone with your daughter?'

'Yes.'

The inspector's eyes narrowed. 'So the father could have taken your child.'

'Oh, no. A woman took her, remember. Someone posing as Rhosyn's grandmother.' Lowri rubbed her eyes in sudden pain. 'I was only out of the shop for ten minutes! All for the sake of a few balloons——'

'Now, now, Miss Morgan,' he said kindly, and told his sergeant to telephone what details they had to the station and to send someone round to question Kay Hooper. 'However,' he said, when they were alone. 'This doesn't rule out the father. The woman could have been working for him.'

Lowri shook her head firmly. 'No. That's out of the question.'

The inspector looked unconvinced. 'Give me his name and address, please.'

Before Lowri could supply it, the phone rang. She jumped to her feet but the sergeant forestalled her.

'We'll see to this,' said the inspector firmly.

'It's a Mr Hawkridge for Miss Morgan,' said the sergeant, Lowri ran to take the receiver from him.

'Lowri?' said Adam, his voice almost unrecognisable. 'For God's sake, what's happening? Any news? Who was that on the phone?'

'The police. Oh, Adam, someone's stolen Rhosyn,' said Lowri shakily.

'Mother told me. I'm in the car right now, on my way. I've tried to get you a couple of times but the line was engaged. Hold on, Lowri—I'll be there as soon as I can.'

Lowri put the receiver down, scrubbed at her face, then sat down again, accepting a cup of coffee gratefully. 'That was Rhosyn's father. I think you can cross him off the list, Inspector, but if you need to question him he'll be here soon.'

'I'd like a few details about him just the same, if you would.'

When Inspector Cox discovered Adam Hawkridge was the head of a successful electronics firm he exchanged a look with the policeman, who sat down by Lowri on the sofa.

'Miss Morgan,' he said gently, 'would Mr Hawkridge be very wealthy by any chance?'

Lowri frowned. 'I don't know.'

The two policemen exchanged looks. 'What do you mean, you don't know?' asked the inspector.

Lowri shrugged. 'He's comfortably off, I suppose. But you'd have to ask him that. Why?' she added suspiciously, then lost every last vestige of colour. 'Oh, I see. Ransom.'

'It's a possibility. Anyone knowing the child's father...'

Lowri shook her head, regaining some of her colour in a rush. 'Hardly anyone does. In fact, until a few days ago only my family knew who Rhosyn's father was.'

'And what happened a few days ago?' probed the inspector.

Lowri explained the accidental meeting, and subsequent discovery by Adam that he possessed a daughter. 'I kept the baby a secret from him for—for reasons of my own.'

'If those reasons throw any light on her disappearance, we need to know them, Miss Morgan.'

'I had no wish to marry Mr Hawkridge,' said Lowri woodenly, 'and saw no reason to inform him of Rhosyn's birth.'

'By which I take it you are not on good terms with Mr Hawkridge,' commented the inspector.

'I wouldn't say that. I had dinner with him at the Chesterton only recently,' she said with perfect truth, then suddenly lost her temper. 'But why are we just sitting here chatting? Why aren't you out there *doing* something about getting my baby back? She'll be in a terrible state, crying for me——' She broke down, crying wildly, and the policewoman put an arm round Lowri, trying to comfort her while the inspector explained as succinctly as possible that a missing child was treated with top priority. The photographs were being copied and would be circulated, and an appeal broadcast on both radio and television later that night. Everything humanly possible would be done to reunite Rhosyn with her mother at top speed.

At the sound of the doorbell Lowri leapt to her feet expectantly, her eyes dulling as the sergeant came into the room to say a Mrs Frances Hobbs and Miss Jenny Hooper were asking to come up.

'Mrs Hobbs is my partner, Miss Hooper runs the crèche.' Lowri subsided, mopping her face. 'Please let them in.'

Jenny rushed in ahead of Fran, ignoring the police as she threw herself into Lowri's arms, begging her forgiveness. 'I should never have gone off and left Kay on her own today; I wouldn't have let Rhosyn out of my sight. Oh, Lowri, I'm so sorry!'

Given the task of calming Jenny down, Lowri pulled herself together, assuring Jenny she wasn't to blame. 'How's Kay?'

'I've left her with my mother. She hasn't stopped crying—she's in a terrible state.'

'Did you contact Rhosyn's grandmother?' asked Fran.

'Yes.'

'What was that?' asked Inspector Cox.

'Since the woman who took Rhosyn pretended to be her grandmother I naturally contacted Mrs Alice Hawkridge first before ringing you,' explained Lowri. 'She lives in Sussex,' she added. 'It was she who contacted Adam to give him the news.'

'I see. And there's no possibility that it could have been *your* mother, Miss Morgan?'

'My mother died ten years ago.'

'I'm sorry.' The inspector moved to the door. 'I'll get back to the station with Sergeant Boyce. WPC Porter will stay here with you for the time being. Overnight if you'd prefer. Try not to worry too much. We'll do everything in our power to get your child back, Miss Morgan.'

When the men had gone, Maggie, as she asked to be called, volunteered to make coffee for everyone, including sandwiches if Lowri would give her run of the kitchen.

'Good idea,' said Fran firmly. 'You must eat something, Lowri.'

Finding it easier to give in than to argue, Lowri nodded listlessly, deeply grateful for her friends' company. Then she jumped up in alarm. 'What am I thinking of? I've got to ring my father and Sarah before they see the news on television.' She shuddered. 'It all seems so much worse when it's put-into words. How could anybody *do* this?'

By the time both phone calls were made Lowri was white and shaking and causing her friends considerable concern.

'Come and eat a sandwich,' said Fran sternly. 'It won't do Rosie any good to come home to a mother in a state of collapse.'

Oddly comforted by Fran's no-nonsense manner, Lowri nibbled at a sandwich, and even managed a smile for Maggie, who had cut crusts off and found a pretty plate for the sandwiches.

'Do you do a lot of this sort of thing?' Lowri asked, as she sipped her coffee.

'Only once before on this type of case, and that's twice too many. But don't worry,' she added staunchly. 'We'll get her back. Inspector Cox is a family man himself. He understands what you're going through. He won't rest until your baby's safe.'

Jenny and Fran assured Lowri that the following day, Christmas Eve or not, they could manage without her at the shop. 'You won't want to be down there to-morrow,' said Jenny.

'I'd rather keep busy,' said Lowri quickly.

'But you may get a lot of nosy parkers coming in just to look at you if you're on the news tonight,' Jenny pointed out unhappily.

When the doorbell rang all three of them waited, tense, as Maggie went out to see who it was. 'It's Mr Hawkridge,' she announced, coming back into the room. 'He's on his way up.'

But Lowri was already on her feet and running out into the hall to open the door at the head of the stairs as Adam came leaping up to meet her. She took one look at his drawn, ashen face, and all her hostility and resentment towards him vanished as though they'd never been. She threw herself into his arms and he crushed her close, rubbing his cheek against hers.

He put Lowri away from him at last, staring down into her tear-stained face. 'No news?'

She shook her head forlornly, and filled him in on what the police were doing so far. 'They thought you might have had something to do with it,' she told him bluntly.

Adam shrugged out of his overcoat. 'Did you?'

'No.'

He breathed in deeply. 'Thank God for that, at least.' He put his arm round her and opened the sitting-room door, then stopped dead at the sight of so many women.

Lowri made the necessary introductions and Fran and Jenny, after a few moments' conversation, began putting coats on, begging Lowri to let them know the minute there was any news.

'Don't worry,' said Adam decisively. 'I'll do all that.' He turned to the policewoman. 'I shall stay here tonight, Constable, so if you need to get back to the station?'

Maggie Porter nodded. 'Right, sir. I'll inform Inspector Cox you're here. He wants to ask you some questions.'

Adam exchanged a glance with Lowri. 'I may as well get that over right away—perhaps your friends could hang on until I get back.'

Fran and Jenny were only too pleased to be of help. When Adam had gone off with Maggie they both turned to Lowri in awe.

'*That's* Rosie's father?' said Fran.

Lowri nodded. 'Yes.'

Jenny gave a low whistle. 'In that case we leave you in good hands, Lowri. He looks equal to anything. I'd hate to be the woman who stole Rosie when he catches up with her.'

Half an hour later Adam returned, and Fran and Jenny went home, promising to be in earlier than usual in the morning.

'Now do you feel?' asked Adam.

'The same as you look, I imagine,' she said bleakly. 'You missed supper with your mother. Shall I cook you bacon and eggs or something?'

'Don't bother.' Adam lifted the cover from the plate of sandwiches. 'I'll have some of these. But I must ring Mother first.'

'Of course.' Lowri tried to smile. 'Please apologise for my hysterics on the phone.'

Adam touched a hand to her pale cheek. 'Under the circumstances she'd have found it strange if you were calm!'

Later, when Adam had spoken to his mother, and Lowri had made yet another pot of coffee, he pulled her down beside him on the sofa.

'Come and sit here, Lowri; we both need human contact,' he said grimly, as he took her hand. 'I've only seen Rhosyn once and I'm berserk with worry. God knows how you must be feeling.'

'I just keep praying that woman's kind,' said Lowri unsteadily, and swallowed hard. 'Rhosyn gets a lot of cuddling—from Jenny and Fran as well as me, not to mention from all the Morgan clan. She's only known love and kindness.'

'Don't!' said Adam roughly, and put his arm round her. 'At least we know some woman's got her. It isn't as though she's lost, or....' He halted, and breathed in deeply as he held her close. 'Have you told your father?'

'Yes. And Sarah. Rhia's in Gstaad with the girls and Mari-Sian. Sarah will contact them when—when——'

'When Rhosyn's back with us,' he said emphatically.

Us? thought Lowri, then leapt to her feet in sudden hope as the telephone rang. Her disappointment was so intense that she felt sick as she listened to Sergeant Boyce informing her there would be an item on the news at nine, and later at ten. There would also be regular radio bulletins asking for information.

When Lowri asked Adam to fetch her television from the spartan little bedroom they sat close together in front of it, waiting tensely for the news.

'You realise what this will mean?' said Lowri dully. 'It's an end to the crèche. No one will ever leave a child with me again after this.'

'In which case you branch out in some other direction,' said Adam the businessman, but his eyes were tender as he turned her face up to his. 'The only thing that matters is to get Rhosyn back. After the newscast someone, somewhere is bound to remember seeing her.'

Lowri's teeth bit into her trembling lower lip. She let out a deep, despairing sigh. 'Oh, Adam, I pray you're right.'

CHAPTER ELEVEN

AFTER the television newscast there were calls from Lowri's father and Rupert, both of them deeply shaken after seeing Rhosyn's photograph. Adam answered them both, Rupert unsurprised to hear his voice, Geraint Morgan too worried over the plight of his granddaughter to question Adam Hawkridge's presence in his daughter's life again.

'Did Dad understand why I couldn't speak to him?' said Lowri, hoarse from weeping.

'I told him you were shattered after watching the news,' said Adam, and stood looking down at her as she huddled in misery on the sofa. 'Why don't you lie down for a bit—get some rest.'

She glared at him. 'Rest? Don't be stupid!' She bit her lip. 'Sorry——'

'Don't be.' He touched a hand to her untidy hair. 'If you won't go to bed, have a bath. Try to relax a little if you can, Lowri.'

She consented reluctantly. 'All right. I'd like to change my clothes, I'll admit.' She gazed up at him imploringly. 'Call me if...'

Adam pulled her to her feet and turned her towards the door. 'Go. I need to make a couple of phone calls, then I'll make you some tea.'

Lowri gave him a pallid little smile and went off to run a bath. While she lay in it for a few minutes she heard his voice, and wondered if he wanted her out of the way so he could talk to someone in private. Adam had said there were no women in his life these days, but she found that hard to believe. Men like Adam needed

146

women like they needed oxygen and food. Pain suddenly struck her like a shaft of lightning. All *she* needed was to have her baby back in her arms again.

Wearing warm grey trousers and a thick scarlet sweater, Lowri emerged to find Adam waiting for her in the sitting room, a tea-tray on the small table beside him.

'I rang the police, then Mother again, to keep her posted, then I got in touch with Jim Wallace to give him this number,' Adam told her at once. 'He's my PA,' he added in response to her questioning look.

So it hadn't been a woman.

'What did the police say?'

'After the news they had several calls from people who'd seen a well-dressed, elderly lady carrying a child into a car near your shop.'

'A car,' repeated Lowri, swallowing. 'So she could be anywhere.'

'If the child was Rhosyn, yes. Descriptions varied somewhat.'

'I told the police what she was wearing, but she was indoors all day up to then. She didn't have a coat, so the woman could have wrapped her in a blanket or something.'

Adam shook his head. 'That would have been noticeable. She probably had something ready for Rhosyn to wear.'

Lowri drew in a deep, shuddering breath. 'So you think it was all premeditated?'

'It sounds like it. Women snatch babies from prams on impulse, but this has all the hallmarks of a well-thought-out plan.'

Lowri poured tea with an unsteady hand. 'You don't think——?' She stopped, hating to put her thought into words.

Adam took the teapot from her shaking hand and put it back on the tray, then sat beside her. 'Think what, Lowri?'

'That the woman intends selling Rhosyn to some couple too desperate for a baby to ask questions?'

He took her hand in a cruel grip. 'We're not even going to think of that one. But even if it's true, we'll find her. I promise you. At least,' he added, 'there's been no ransom demand so far.'

Lowri stared at him blankly. 'How do you know?'

'That's why I rang Jim Wallace. Nothing's come in at the office, anyway. In the meantime he's going round to my flat to check my messages. He'll ring later.'

'Why is your PA a man?' asked Lowri curiously.

'When my father abdicated, his assistant resigned.'

'Didn't she want to work for you?'

'She was a married lady who left because she was pregnant,' said Adam without expression. 'At the time I was still licking the wounds you'd inflicted, and ill disposed towards women in general. So I hired a man. It works well. Jim's highly qualified, dependable, and never objects to working late.'

'Any of which could apply to a woman just as well,' snapped Lowri.

'Good girl!' Adam smiled. 'I'd rather you ripped at me than wept. Your tears cut me to pieces.'

In which case, thought Lowri morosely, it was a pity she hadn't turned them on him full force when she'd first found out she was pregnant.

'I just wish we could hear something,' she said miserably.

Adam hooked her close with a long arm. 'I know, I know.'

'I just keep picturing her crying for me, Adam. The woman won't know what she eats, or what milk I give her, or—or anything.' She burrowed her head into his shoulder, utterly oblivious of him as a man. For the moment he just represented comfort she needed so badly that she forgot that he'd ever been her lover.

Adam, however, shifted restlessly after a while, and she detached herself quickly and sat erect in the corner of the sofa.

'I could do with a drink,' he said tightly. 'A pity you keep a dry house, Lowri.'

'The Green Man down the road is probably still open, if you're desperate.'

'Not that desperate.' He gave her a hard look. 'Alcohol, at least, has never been a problem for me.'

'Unlike women.' She gave him a sidelong glance. 'At one time the problem was a glut; nowadays it's a dearth.'

'Both circumstances solely by choice,' he reminded her cuttingly, then raised his hand in apology. 'Sorry. I'm on edge.'

'We both are,' she agreed, sighing, then her eyes narrowed. 'Wait a minute.' She sprang up and went into her bedroom, and came back waving a miniature barrel of cognac. 'How about this?'

Adam looked amused. 'Where did that come from?'

'I put it in my father's Christmas stocking.' Lowri tried to smile. 'I can easily get something else if—when——'

'When!' said Adam promptly, and jumped to his feet to take the barrel from her. 'Right. We'll both have some.'

Normally Lowri loathed spirits, but tonight she was in sore need of any help she could get to ward off the panic and grief she was holding at bay only by supreme effort of will.

'Better?' asked Adam, as she sipped cautiously.

'The effect, yes. I hate the taste.'

He smiled, and topped up their glasses. 'Neither of us will get drunk on this amount. But it might make the waiting marginally more bearable.'

The night wore on at such a snail's pace that Lowri was glad of the inner, transient warmth derived from the brandy. Jim Wallace rang to relay the messages on Adam's phone, but no demand for ransom had been among them. The only other phone call came from Inspector Cox just before midnight to say that, while they had several eye-witness reports of the child being driven off in a car, nothing more could be done until morning. More appeals would be broadcast on breakfast television, after which there might be more leads to go on. He told Adam to advise Miss Morgan to get some rest and promised to be in touch the moment they had any news.

'How does he expect me to rest in these circumstances?' said Lowri in despair.

'You might sleep if you went to bed.'

She shook her head positively. 'I just don't want to be on my own——' She flushed, and Adam smiled mockingly.

'Don't worry. I know that wasn't an invitation. We'll just sit here and talk all night, if you like.' His eyes met hers. 'Whatever you want, I'll do, Lowri.'

She inclined her head gravely. 'Thank you.'

They resumed their places on the sofa. And this time when Adam put his arm round her Lowri leaned against him gratefully, thankful for the warmth and rock-like security of his hold.

'I haven't thanked you for all the presents you sent,' she said in sudden remorse. 'I forgot.'

'Did Rhosyn like the rocking horse?'

'She certainly did. Much excitement! Very extravagant of you—or did you decide on something as big as that so I couldn't send it back?'

He laughed a little. 'Something like that.'

'She hasn't seen the teddy yet——' Lowri swallowed hard on a sudden gush of tears. She cleared her throat. 'The clothes are beautiful. Did you choose them?'

'No. I wouldn't have known where to start. My mother did that.'

Lowri stiffened. 'You—you told her about Rhosyn, then.'

'Yes.'

'Why?'

'Why not?'

Lowri would have drawn away, but Adam's arm tightened to prevent her.

'How did she react?' she asked after a while.

Adam rubbed his chin with his free hand. 'She couldn't believe it at first.'

'That Rhosyn was yours?'

'No, that she actually had a grandchild. She couldn't believe her luck.'

Lowri screwed her head round to look up at him narrowly. 'Luck? I trust you made it clear you've got no claim on Rhosyn?'

His face hardened. 'I did. But my mother still thinks of her as her granddaughter!'

Lowri subsided, deflated. 'Yes, of course. If—when I get Rhosyn back, your mother's welcome to come and visit her.'

'How about me?' he said swiftly.

There was silence for a moment.

'Let's get Rhosyn back first,' she said gruffly. 'Until then I can't think about—about anything else.'

Another silence.

After a while Adam said casually, 'Did you receive the other package?'

Lowri flushed with embarrassment. 'Oh—yes. Sorry! I should have thanked you for that, too.'

'I wasn't asking for thanks.' He stared at his shoes morosely. 'I was collecting a ring my mother'd sent to a jeweller for enlarging, and the brooch caught my eye. I bought it for you on impulse.'

'It's lovely. I don't have much jewellery. Thank you,' said Lowri, who up to that moment hadn't decided whether she'd keep the brooch or not. But to hand it back to Adam under the present circumstances seemed hardly the thing to do.

'I thought it would serve as a reminder of happier days,' said Adam very quietly.

Lowri nodded silently. 'I haven't bought anything for you,' she said after a while.

He gave a mirthless laugh. 'I didn't imagine you would. Every time you look at Rhosyn you must curse the day you ever laid eyes on me.'

'Good heavens, no!' She looked up at him in astonishment. 'You've seen Rhosyn. How could I possibly regret anything to do with her? Any animosity I feel towards you, Adam, is for a quite different reason.'

His eyes hardened. 'You don't have to spell it out, Lowri. It's obvious that marriage to me was such an unbearable prospect that you chose the life of a single parent in preference to it.'

This was by no means accurate, but Lowri was in no mood to explain. 'Let's not talk about it,' she said shortly.

He took her at her word. The silence between them lengthened to such an extent that to her guilty surprise Lowri found herself growing drowsy. Her eyelids drooped and she blinked them open, horrified that she could even think of sleeping when Rhosyn was somewhere out there in the cold night with strangers. As he felt her deep, shuddering sigh Adam's arm tightened, his free hand stroked her hair in wordless sympathy and Lowri's body relaxed against his even as her brain ordered her to keep alert. The tension and anguish of the past few hours took their toll, and as the endless night wore on towards morning sleep overwhelmed her and granted her the boon of an hour or two's oblivion.

When Lowri woke she was stiff and cold, and alone on the sofa. Adam was nowhere to be seen. Frowning, she staggered to the bathroom, then recoiled in horror at the sight of his naked body in the bath. She shot back out again, blushing scarlet at the amusement she saw—belatedly—in his eyes.

She went into the kitchen and leaned her head on her arms on a counter top, her embarrassment obliterated as the misery of Rhosyn's absence swept over her in a tide. After a while she pulled herself together, washed her face under the kitchen tap and filled the kettle. By the time Adam joined her, his hair damp and his jaw dark with stubble, she'd made tea and was slicing bread to put in the toaster.

'Good morning,' she said, not looking at him. 'Would you like some eggs?'

'Good morning—and I'd like some eggs very much.' He pulled a face. 'One's appetite functions separately from the mind, apparently. I thought I wouldn't be able to face food in the circumstances, but apart from those sandwiches I didn't eat anything yesterday——'

'Then you must be starving! Give me a minute to wash and I'll make you an omelette.' Lowri disappeared to wash and tidy herself up, eyeing her pallid face and dark-ringed eyes with distaste. She brushed her hair, tied it back and returned to the kitchen, where Adam was drinking coffee. 'Make one for me, please,' she said casually, and put an omelette pan on the cooker.

'Let's eat breakfast in the other room,' said Adam, handing over a mug. 'It's almost time for a television newscast.'

Lowri nodded silently, swallowed some coffee, then broke eggs into a bowl. She added some herbs and seasoning, poured the mixture into the sizzling pan, and within minutes they were side by side again on the sofa, the tray on a table in front of them. They had finished eating by the time Rhosyn's photograph appeared on the screen, something Lowri was thankful for. One look at her daughter's face tightened her throat so painfully that it was some time before she could drink her coffee.

'We didn't talk about her last night,' said Adam suddenly. 'Tell me about Rhosyn—everything about her.'

Lowri gave him a startled glance, then decided he was right. 'Where shall I start?'

'With her birth. Was it hard?'

Lowri shrugged. 'It wasn't fun, but it was normal enough. She took twelve hours to arrive, by which time I'd had quite enough of the whole process. But one look at her and all the pain and effort was worth it.'

'Was she big?'

'Eight and a half pounds.' Lowri grimaced. 'I wouldn't like to produce a bigger baby, believe me.'

'Do you intend to do that?' said Adam quickly.

Lowri gave him a baleful look. 'None of your business,' she snapped.

There was a hostile pause.

'Was she a good baby?' Adam asked eventually.

'Yes, she was. From about six weeks old she slept all night most nights, except when she was teething or had the sniffles.'

'So how old was she when you started on this place?'

'Three months. And at first I was so tired I thought I'd bitten off more than I could chew. But I coped.' Lowri smiled ruefully. 'My father was convinced I wasn't up to it, and I was determined to show him I could. And I have. It's the ideal business to run with a baby, remember. And I've had Fran's experience to lean on, and then we took on Jenny, which means I make a late start, take a long lunch hour with Rhosyn, and when she's two she'll go to nursery school——'

'As young as that?' he said, startled.

'Oh, yes. It's all fixed up. It's a bit expensive, but it's a Montessori-type school, where they have French lessons, and ballet, too, if you like, only it's extra...' Lowri trailed away, her eyes haunted.

Adam pushed the table away so he could take her in his arms. 'We'll get her back,' he said hoarsely into her hair. 'Only for God's sake don't look like that.'

They clung together convulsively then jumped apart as the phone rang, and kept on ringing at intervals all morning. First it was Geraint Morgan, then Sarah, then Alice Hawkridge, after which Inspector Cox reported that the police were doing house-to-house questioning in the area, showing Rhosyn's photograph.

Jenny and Fran arrived early, asking what help was necessary, apart from manning the shop.

'Stay up here while I go shopping,' said Adam, and smiled at the amazement on Lowri's face. 'I didn't bring any luggage, remember, I need some shirts and so on, and a razor.'

'Don't be long,' said Lowri involuntarily, and flushed as he squeezed her hand.

'Direct me to the nearest shop and I'll be half an hour at the most.'

After he left practical Fran saw to the dishes, while Jenny apologised on Kay's behalf yet again.

'She asked to come and help today, but I knew that's the last thing you'd want——'

'Why?' said Lowri. 'For one thing I doubt you'll get any customers for the crèche today after what's happened. But if Kay wants to come and give a hand in the shop I think it's a good idea. It's Christmas Eve, remember. Besides,' she added, pressing Jenny's hand, 'Kay will feel a lot better if she helps. It wasn't her fault. I really don't blame her—she wasn't to know.'

Jenny hugged Lowri's hand. 'It's so *good* of you. I'll give her a ring right now.'

By the time Adam returned the shop was open and Jenny and a pathetically grateful Kay were manning it while Fran stayed with Lowri, her sane, practical presence doing a lot to keep her partner on an even keel.

Fran got up to let him in, smiling wrily at his load of packages. 'Father Christmas, I presume! I'll go down, then. Chin up, Lowri.'

When they were alone Lowri eyed the bags askance. 'I thought you'd only gone to buy a shirt.'

'I bought more than one, also the necessary equipment to shave, since your bathroom was innocent of razors——'

'I've got a little electric thing you could have used if you'd asked.' Lowri peered into a large carrier bag. 'And this is full of food!' she said accusingly.

'There isn't much in your kitchen,' he pointed out.

'I know. I haven't done much shopping lately because we—we were going away tonight——' Lowri turned away, determined not to cry. 'I'll put this stuff away. You can use my bedroom to change.'

'Sorry I was so long, by the way,' he said as he picked up the bags. 'My favourite caterer's foodhall was like a rugby scrum. Good thing I was there as they opened. But at least I got most of my shopping done under one roof.'

Lowri managed a smile. 'Do you usually wear chainstore shirts?'

'All the time,' he lied shamelessly. 'How about some coffee?'

Business downstairs was brisk all morning; not in the crèche, as expected, but otherwise the shop was busy. There were a few curious people eager to see the bereft mother, Fran reported, but there were a lot of genuine customers hunting for last-minute bargains; also some of their regular customers had come in, eager to offer sympathy. Two of these had given valuable information about the elderly lady seen taking a young child into a car. One young woman remembered the make of the car, and the other described the yellow wind cheater the child was wearing, also the obvious difficulty the woman had in fastening the little girl into the car seat.

'At least she had Rhosyn safe in a proper seat,' said Lowri, determined to be positive.

Fran nodded. 'Which means she'll be taking care of Rosie properly. By the way,' she added as she went to the door, 'I've had a couple of offers for the rocking horse. I turned them down, of course.'

'I should hope so,' retorted Lowri, avoiding Adam's eye.

The morning seemed endless, though to the impartial onlooker the scene was oddly domesticated as Adam read the newspaper he'd brought and Lowri dealt with the large basket of ironing she was never without. They drank endless cups of coffee, but neither of them had any appetite for the cookies and buns Adam had bought earlier, though Fran and her cohorts were grateful for them as lunchtime approached, as none of the three would hear of leaving the shop for lunch or any other reason.

Phone calls kept coming in, some of them with sympathy from local business people, others from Sarah and Holly, both of them unable to wait in silence for news, and towards midday Alice Hawkridge rang again, and after a brief conversation with her son this time asked to speak to Lowri.

'I just wanted to say I'm praying for you—hard,' said Adam's mother firmly. 'And I've told Adam he's to try and get you to eat.'

Lowri managed a little laugh. 'He does that constantly. He's been quite overbearing about it.'

There was a pause. 'Try not to be too hard on him, my dear.'

'Mrs Hawkridge, if—no, *when* I get Rhosyn back I don't think I'll ever be hard on anyone again for the rest of my life!'

'Then I'll pray even harder. And now I'll ring off to keep your line free.'

Lunchtime came and went, by which time Adam had given up all attempt to make Lowri eat. As time passed she became more and more tense, finding it hard to make any attempt at conversation, and Adam, in no better state, gave up trying to lighten her mood. Suddenly, halfway through the afternoon, Lowri buried her head in her hands and gave way to bitter tears, and Adam seized her and rocked her in his arms. When she raised a swollen, tear-stained face to his at last, Adam kissed her quivering mouth gently and smoothed her hair back from her damp forehead.

'Don't give up, Lowri.'

She detached herself and sat up straight. 'Sorry. It just came over me in a wave all of a sudden. I must look a fright. I'll go and do something to myself.'

When she returned, with a touch of make up on her newly washed face, Adam eyed her in approval.

'That's my girl.' He bit his lip at her quizzical look. 'Purely a figure of speech, Lowri.'

'Of course.' She gave a determined little smile. 'No more tears, I promise. I don't usually cry much, you know.'

'No,' said Adam bluntly, 'I don't know. You never gave me the chance to find out.'

'True.' For some reason she felt in command of herself again. 'Now I think I could manage one of those buns you bought——' She broke off as the phone rang and raced out of the room to answer it.

'Miss Morgan? Cox here.'

'Inspector! Any news?'

'Don't get your hopes too high, but it's possible I might have. If we come round now we can take you to an address we've been given.'

Lowri gasped. 'You've found Rhosyn? Where is she? Who's got her——?'

'Miss Morgan, calm down. We don't know anything concrete yet. But we need you with us to identify a child.'

Lowri went cold, sagging against Adam. '*Identify*? What are you saying?'

'Nothing sinister. This child we've heard about is alive and well, I promise you. But I must stress that there's no guarantee that it's your child.'

As Lowri put the phone down Adam grabbed her hands. 'Well?' he demanded, his eyes blazing in his haggard face.

'They're coming to collect me——'

'You're not going without me!'

She nodded impatiently. 'Of course not!' She repeated Inspector Cox's news. 'He sounded a bit cagey—doesn't want to commit himself. Will you tell the girls?'

Adam raced down to the shop, then came back up the stairs two at a time and grabbed Lowri to him. 'Don't build too much on this, darling!'

'How can I not?' she said wildly, then breathed in deeply and pulled herself together. 'You're right, of course. But it's so *hard*, Adam.'

'Bloody hard!' He held her coat for her. 'Put a scarf on, or something. It's cold out there.'

When Sergeant Boyce came to collect them Lowri and Adam were in the hall, waiting, Lowri still as a statue, Adam pacing up and down like a caged tiger.

'Not far to go,' Inspector Cox assured them as they joined him in the car. 'The message came from one of those pricey flats in Gloucester Place.'

'Do you think it's Rhosyn?' said Adam urgently, before Lowri could speak.

'The man who rang thinks it is. He sounded in a bit of a state. Just asked me to come as quickly as possible. We'll soon see.'

When the car drew up outside a block of imposing luxury flats Adam helped Lowri out, keeping his arm about her as they went up in a lift with the inspector. In tense silence they went out into a hall where the inspector rang the bell of one of the four doors leading off it.

A haggard man opened the door to admit them, looking utterly distraught. Inspector Cox introduced himself and his companions.

'My name's Charles Blanchard,' the man said as he showed them into a comfortably furnished room overlooking well-tended gardens. 'Could I just explain a little before you see the baby? She's perfectly safe, I swear.' He looked from Lowri to Adam despairingly. 'I can't apologise enough for what's happened. I can hardly take it in—I arrived only a short time ago to fetch my mother to spend Christmas with us. I'd seen the photographs of the missing baby on television last night, so you can imagine my horror when my mother handed the very same child over to me, saying she'd found the perfect Christmas present for us.'

'Please, Mr Blanchard, don't keep me in suspense,' broke in Lowri, unable to bear it a moment longer. 'Where is my baby?'

'I'll take you to her now,' said Charles Blanchard in quick remorse. 'She fell asleep, so I asked a neighbour to sit with her while I made arrangements for my mother—who's in a state of mental collapse. She's been hospitalised. Her doctor went with her, and I'll follow on once everything's sorted out here. Forgive me, but it's been hell on wheels this last hour or two. Will you come this way?'

Adam's grasp was cruelly tight on Lowri's hand as they followed Charles Blanchard to a small room where an elderly woman rose quickly from beside the cot, the sudden movement disturbing the sleeping child. The little girl's swollen eyes opened, then lit up like stars at the sight of her mother.

'Mum-mum-mum-mum!' cried Rhosyn, stretching up her arms, and Lowri swept her up in a fierce embrace, rubbing her cheek over and over again against the small head, hardly able to believe she had her baby safe. Then Adam's arms closed round them both, confirming beyond all doubt that this was actually happening, that the nightmare was really over.

CHAPTER TWELVE

IT WAS late that night when Rhosyn was finally, happily asleep in her own cot again. All the jubilant, thankful phone calls had been made and interviews given to the local television news team as well as a perky young cub reporter from the *Pennington Weekly Chronicle*.

'Won't come out until next week,' said the young man cheerfully, 'but it'll still be good news. Just the stuff for the festive season.'

Fran, Jenny and Kay went home by taxi at last, all three of them jubilant, and intoxicated more by thankfulness and sheer fatigue than the champagne Adam bought to celebrate Rhosyn's return.

The feisty little girl recovered from her adventure with remarkable speed, other than a tendency to cling round her mother's neck now and again, and responded to Adam's subtle advances with a flirtatious enthusiasm he all too plainly found irresistible. By the time her baby daughter had played with all her familiar toys, and had been bathed and fed and cuddled to sleep, Lowri felt exhausted, the adrenaline deserting her in a rush once the flat was quiet and she was alone with Adam.

Adam looked at his watch. 'It's late. I'd better make a move——'

'You're not driving back to London at this time of night?' said Lowri in dismay. 'You haven't eaten, and there was the champagne——'

'Only one glass, Lowri,' he said brusquely, not looking at her. 'Besides, I don't have much alternative. It's Christmas Eve, remember. There'll be no room at the inn locally at such short notice.'

162

'But you can sleep here! There's a single bed in Rhosyn's room. I'll take that and you can have mine.' Lowri put out a hand in entreaty, finding she hated the thought of being alone. 'Couldn't you drive back to London in the morning? Please? You can still be with your mother in good time for lunch.'

Adam looked at her long and hard. 'Why, Lowri? Is this a need for *my* company, or a simple dislike of solitude after all you've been through?'

'Some of both,' she said honestly, and smiled in entreaty. 'Now the holiday plans are changed I thought perhaps you'd like to see Rhosyn open her Christmas stocking in the morning before we set off——'

'In different directions,' said Adam expressionlessly and put out a hand to turn her face up to his. 'Does this mean you've had a change of heart, Lowri?'

'As far as you and Rhosyn are concerned, yes.'

'But nothing more than that.'

Lowri met his eyes squarely. 'No other change of heart, certainly.'

'You mean you still hate the sight of me,' he said bitterly.

'You know that's not true!'

'Do I?'

They looked at each other in silence, then Lowri pocketed her pride. 'Please stay, Adam. I can't bear the thought of being alone tonight. I badly need someone to talk to until this feeling of helplessness recedes a bit.'

He smiled mirthlessly. 'You're honest.'

'You bought a lot of food and we've hardly eaten any of it. And there's some champagne left. Let's have a meal and celebrate Rhosyn's return together.'

'Put like that, how can I refuse?'

Lowri smiled at him with radiant gratitude. 'You listen for Rhosyn,' she ordered. 'I'll throw something together in the kitchen.'

'Can I help?'

'I'll manage better on my own——' She caught herself up, flushing.

'As usual!'

Lowri retreated hurriedly, and shut herself in the kitchen, away from the searching eyes that had haunted her dreams so often during the long, lonely months of their estrangement.

Half an hour later she called him to the small table she'd set with a checked cloth and red candles in saucers wreathed with holly. She'd cooked rice, concocted a tomato sauce fragrant with herbs and garlic and added the king prawns Adam bought to it, defrosted a loaf of wholemeal bread and accompanied it with a slab of her favourite Caerphilly cheese to complete the line-up. Adam exclaimed in surprise as she showed him to his chair with a flourish. 'Impressive—and fast!'

'I aim to please,' she said demurely.

'Not always——' he began, then threw up a hand in apology. 'Sorry. Tonight let's just forget certain bits of the past and concentrate on the pleasanter aspects of our relationship.'

'Right,' said Lowri quickly, not sure this was too wise a move. For her some of the most memorable and blissful time had been spent in his bed, a thought which struck Adam simultaneously she suspected, as colour rose along his cheekbones.

'This is wonderful,' he said, mouth full, and smiled across the candle-flames at her. 'Until this minute I didn't know I was starving.'

'Me too,' she agreed, and for a while there was a companionable silence while they tucked into the meal. But a little later, once the first edge was off her appetite, Lowri gave a sigh. 'I can't help feeling sorry for that poor woman, you know.'

'Mrs Blanchard?' said Adam, and nodded gravely. 'I know. She's obviously mentally disturbed, and now Rhosyn's safe it's difficult to condemn her. In her own mind she was just giving her son the one Christmas present he and his wife wanted most.'

'Poor thing. I keep seeing that little room with the cot and those toys—it was heartbreaking.'

While Lowri was dressing Rhosyn Adam had been present when the police questioned Charles Blanchard, who said that his mother had suffered a nervous breakdown after the death of his father a few months previously. He'd genuinely believed she was fully recovered, and blamed himself bitterly for letting his mother know when his wife miscarried a few weeks earlier. Charles Blanchard was the father of two healthy sons, Lowri learned to her relief, but admitted that his mother had a fixation about a granddaughter, never dreaming she'd take matters into her own hands to provide one by such disastrous means.

'A pity the police had to be involved,' said Lowri with regret.

'If they hadn't been, Blanchard wouldn't have seen Rhosyn's photograph. But at least there's no question of his mother being charged, now Blanchard's committed her to proper professional care.'

'Poor woman,' Lowri sighed. 'And all this happened just because I went out for balloons. Fran says she must have been in the store-room getting out more shoes for the child she was fitting, which is why no one noticed when Rhosyn was spirited away. My daughter thought it was one big game, probably.'

'Perhaps it was fate,' commented Adam, pouring the last of the champagne into their glasses.

'Pretty cruel if it was!'

'Now Rhosyn's safe I can't feel it was total cruelty where I'm concerned, if I'm honest.' His eyes locked with hers, bright and unwavering over the candle flames. 'Nothing else would have compelled you to contact me, Lowri, would it?'

Her eyes fell. 'Possibly not.'

'Which brings me to something you said earlier. My mother, you promised, would be welcome to visit Rhosyn, but what about me?' Adam reached a hand across the table to capture hers. 'Like it or not, I am Rhosyn's father, Lowri.'

'If you'd shown more enthusiasm for the idea from the start I'd be more sympathetic,' she retorted. Her chin lifted. 'To be accused of trapping a man into marriage is a pretty difficult thing to forget. Or forgive.'

Adam released her hand and sat back, his face hidden in the shadow beyond the candlelight. 'It was said in the heat of the moment, at a time when life was throwing quite a lot at me, one way and another. Now I can't think why the thought ever crossed my mind, but if it makes you feel any better I've paid for it ever since, one way and another. Haven't *you* ever said anything you regret, Lowri?'

'I regret the thing I didn't say,' she said bitterly, and swallowed the rest of her champagne in one gulp. 'As I mentioned once before, a good old-fashioned no to you in the beginning would have saved us all a lot of trouble.'

'Then there'd be no Rhosyn,' he said swiftly, and Lowri calmed down somewhat as she digested this incontrovertible truth.

'That's one point in your favour, I suppose,' she muttered after a while, and got up. 'You go in the other room while I clear up.'

'No. We'll do it together,' he said decisively, in a tone Lowri didn't dare argue with.

In taut silence they dealt with the detritus of their meal, and afterwards Adam took a tray of coffee into the other room while Lowri went to look at Rhosyn, something she'd been doing at regular intervals all evening, almost unable to credit the miracle of having her child safe once more. Adam came to join her, and in silence they looked down at the flushed, angelic little face together, then without a word he turned away at last and left the room as quietly as he came.

Lowri stayed where she was, her eyes on Rhosyn, but her mind on Rhosyn's father. What did she do now? Allow Adam a visit now and then? But if she did, explanations could be difficult once Rhosyn was old enough to understand why Daddy lived somewhere else. And always had.

The telephone brought her from her reverie, but by the time she got to the hall Adam had answered it.

'It's your father,' he said, handing her the receiver, and went back into the sitting-room, closing the door behind him.

Lowri joined him after a while, and poured coffee for them both in a silence Adam broke after a while as though he could stand it no longer.

'Your father anxious about Rhosyn?' he asked abruptly.

'He was pleased she'd settled down to sleep happily, yes.' Lowri got up from her chair and sat on the sofa beside him. 'Adam, what are you doing tomorrow?'

He frowned. 'Tomorrow?'

Lowri nodded. 'Yes, tomorrow, the twenty-fifth of December, Christmas Day.'

His face set. 'I hadn't forgotten. I'm spending it with my mother, what else?'

Lowri thrust a hand through her hair, coughed, looked away, then in a rush said 'Dad thought—I mean Holly suggested—and if you don't want to they'll understand, so will I, of course, please feel free to refuse——'

'Refuse what, for crying out loud?' Adam said in exasperation.

Lowri took a deep breath. 'The weather forecast is good, and it's not all that far, so Dad thought you might like to drive your mother down to spend the day with us, in Cwmderwen, I mean—to celebrate getting Rhosyn back safely for Christmas.'

A light flared in Adam's eyes. 'Your father's inviting *me*?'

Lowri nodded. 'And your mother.'

Adam gazed at her in silence, a very strange look on his face. 'How about you?'

'Oh, I'll be there too,' she assured him flippantly.

He caught her hands in his. 'You know perfectly well what I'm asking,' he said with sudden violence. 'Do *you* want me there?'

She nodded wordlessly, and he caught her to him and kissed her, and it was so good to feel his mouth on hers with the old, potent hunger Lowri let him go on kissing her and kissed him back. But when she felt the urgency rise in a powerful tide in his body Lowri drew away, shaking her head.

Adam's face set into an expressionless mask. 'So you're still punishing me.'

'No. I'm not. But you can't walk back into my life and expect everything to be the same, Adam.' Lowri got to her feet. 'I don't feel any animosity towards you now—I suppose the past twenty-four hours were something of a lesson in priorities. But when I asked you to stay tonight I made it quite clear it wasn't in my bed.'

'Such an exalted privilege never occurred to me,' he said bitterly, and jumped to his feet. 'All I took—and received—was a kiss, Lowri.'

They stared at each other in a taut, hostile silence broken at last by the sound of church bells.

Adam made a jerky, uncharacteristic gesture. 'It's Christmas, Lowri. Goodwill towards men.'

'Then, since you're indisputedly a man,' she said with a faint, reluctant smile, 'and entitled to goodwill, let's call a truce. Merry Christmas, Adam.' She closed the gap between them and stood on tiptoe to kiss his cheek.

'Merry Christmas,' he responded, and returned the kiss very carefully in kind.

'Now,' said Lowri practically, 'will it frighten your mother to death if you ring her this late? I hope not, because after insisting she joins the Morgans for Christmas you've got to remind her to put the turkey in the freezer.'

Christmas Day was at once the strangest and the most wonderful Lowri had ever spent in her life—and the longest. After only a few hours' sleep she woke Adam very early so he could give Rhosyn the teddy and help her open her Christmas stocking. After a hasty breakfast Lowri sped him on his way to London then dressed her daughter in the dungarees and ski-jacket chosen by Mrs Hawkridge, pinned the cricket brooch to the collar of her new red shirt and set off on the two-hour journey to Cwmderwen.

When she arrived at the familiar house with the sentry-box porch and long, rambling garden, Geraint Morgan appeared in the doorway before Lowri came to a halt. He came sprinting down the path, with Holly following more slowly, holding Huw by the hand, their faces so bright with welcome and love that Lowri had a fight to keep back the tears as she freed Rhosyn from her car seat just in time to be caught in a communal embrace as they all hugged each other, and Geraint Morgan kissed his granddaughter over and over again before hefting her on one arm with his little son on the other, leaving Holly and Lowri to follow him up the path to the house.

Holly Morgan, who was tall and slender, with smudges of fatigue under her dark eyes, kept her arm round Lowri as they stood in the hall watching Geraint help Huw show Rhosyn the tall, brightly lit Christmas tree.

'It's a miracle,' she sighed, her eyes wet. She gave Lowri a searching look. 'How are you—really, I mean? I can see the dark marks under your eyes. We've all got a matching set after that terrible night. But are you feeling all right underneath?'

'I feel wonderful!' said Lowri with truth, and grinned. 'Ready to peel sprouts or baste the turkey, or whatever you like, now you've got two extra visitors to cope with.'

Geraint Morgan, whose powerful build was the kind more associated with a rugby scrum than a solicitor's office, looked up with a smile. 'That was Holly's idea, by the way.'

'You mean you still have reservations about Adam,' countered Lowri.

'Have you?'

Lowri shrugged. 'I don't know what I feel towards Adam, except that whatever it is it's nothing to do with animosity.'

'Then I'll extend true Welsh hospitality to both Adam and Mrs Hawkridge,' said her father firmly. 'In the meantime let's have a medicinal glass of cheer and open the presents before these two do it for us.'

By the time Adam arrived with his mother the sitting-room was a sea of wrapping paper, with two small, excited people playing happily with each other's toys while their elders relaxed under the influence of good sherry and a blazing fire and the sheer joy of being together after the trauma of Rhosyn's disappearance.

Lowri answered the door to the new arrivals, feeling a little tense until she looked into a pair of eyes so like Adam's she felt she knew his mother already. Alice Hawkridge, who was tall, grey-haired and handsome, with a no-nonsense air about her, bridged the awkward moment of meeting by taking Lowri in her arms and giving her a hug.

'Happy Christmas, my dear.'

'Happy Christmas to you, too, Mrs Hawkridge. I'm so glad you could come.' Lowri gave her a radiant smile.

'Nothing would have kept me away once your father was kind enough to include us in your celebration. Now don't keep me in suspense—lead me to my granddaughter!'

Adam, who had changed from his dark city suit into a tweed jacket and cords at some stage in his travels, looked rather weary as he smiled at Lowri. 'As you can see, Mother's priorities are firmly in place.'

Lowri led the way into the sitting-room, which was in such a mess all constraint evaporated as the introductions were made. Geraint Morgan clasped Adam's hand, laughing as Alice Hawkridge, once she'd thanked her hosts, promptly sat down on the floor with a child either side and embarked on a detailed examination of every last toy Rhosyn and Huw presented for her inspection, so obviously delighted Holly had no compunction in leaving her to it as she went off with Lowri to see to the meal.

'Do you think Adam will be all right in there with Dad?' asked Lowri, as she made brandy sauce for the pudding.

'Best to let them get on with it. Besides, your Adam looks well able to take care of himself,' commented Holly as she decanted vegetables into dishes.

'He's not my Adam,' protested Lowri.

'Pull the other one,' snorted her stepmother.

The meal was a lively, convivial affair, with no formality possible when two boisterous, noisy little people in high-chairs were joining in the fun. Alice Hawkridge insisted on seating herself between Huw and Rhosyn, who ate up their turkey and vegetables like little angels, utterly enslaved by this new playmate.

The only sober moment came when Geraint Morgan said grace, giving thanks for the blessing of Rhosyn's return.

'Amen,' said Lowri huskily, and looked up to meet Adam's eyes. She smiled shakily, and began passing the plates as her father carved the turkey.

During the meal Lowri finally relaxed as she saw her father and Adam seemed able to talk together far more easily than she'd expected. And it would have been a very difficult guest indeed who couldn't have got on with Alice Hawkridge.

'More wine, Adam?' said Geraint, proffering a bottle.

'Thank you, no, I'm driving,' said Adam with regret.

Geraint exchanged a look with Holly, who immediately suggested their guests stay the night.

'It might be a bit of a squash,' she said smiling, 'but we can manage if we shift round a bit.'

Adam obviously welcomed the idea, but his mother shook her head.

'You've been wonderfully kind having us here today, and we appreciate it very much indeed, but I think we should go home this evening. You've all had a terrible shock and tonight you'll be tired. The last thing you need is two extra guests for the night.'

'Mother's right,' said Adam at once, and smiled warmly at Holly. 'It's very good of you, but later on you'll be glad of some peace.'

'You'd be very welcome,' said Geraint quietly, and Adam gave him a very direct look.

'Thank you. I appreciate that. Another time we'd be glad to.'

After the big meal the two children were taken off for a nap while the others drank coffee in front of the fire. The conversation turned inevitably to Rhosyn's terrifying adventure, and after a while Holly, sensing signs of restlessness in Adam, turned to Lowri.

'Why don't you take Adam for a walk? Some fresh air before his long drive home might be a good idea.'

Adam sprang to his feet with such alacrity that Lowri had no choice but to follow suit. Her father, misunderstanding her reluctance, smiled at her reassuringly.

'Don't worry, *cariad*—Rhosyn's safe here.'

Lowri smiled. 'I know. And if she wakes up and needs entertaining I'm sure her grandma will be only too happy to oblige.'

There was general laughter, and Mrs Hawkridge nodded briskly, blinking as she sniffed hard.

'Very happy!' she agreed.

Outside in the frosty afternoon Lowri strolled with Adam in rather tense silence along a footpath which took them through the fields to the church.

'Would you like to see inside?' she asked politely. 'My uncle—Sarah's father—was the vicar here.'

'Would you mind if we just walked?' said Adam. 'I need to talk to you, Lowri, and since talking to you invariably leads to argument, a church hardly seems the best place.'

They fell in step again, taking a lane which led through fields crisp with frost.

'You know what I want to talk about,' went on Adam, a determined jut to his chin.

Lowri nodded. 'I assume you want to discuss arrangements for seeing Rhosyn.'

Adam gave her a black look. 'You assume wrong. I already know you intend to let me see Rhosyn. Which makes me very happy. What I'm not so happy about is my standing with you. Am I just to be Rhosyn's father, or are you going to let me back in your life as——'

'As what?' asked Lowri crisply.

They paused by a stile.

'I wish,' said Adam harshly, 'that I could go back in time and start again at the moment you announced you were pregnant.'

'But, since you can't, we just have to deal with things the way they are.' Lowri looked up at him in appeal. 'Let's not spoil Christmas Day, Adam, I need time. Surely you can understand that?'

'I thought we'd wasted enough time already,' he said bitterly. 'I hoped that after what we've been through together these past few days you'd softened towards me. Obviously I was mistaken.'

Lowri put a hand on his arm. 'No, you weren't. But neither of us is functioning normally at the moment——'

'I am,' he broke in swiftly, and pulled her into his arms, kissing her hungrily, his hold quelling her instinctive bid for freedom. When he raised his head at last he smiled crookedly into her upturned, scarlet face. 'I deserved one kiss, Lowri.'

'And one kiss is all you'll get,' she retorted, thoroughly irritable because her heart was thumping and she badly wanted to throw herself back in his arms and let him kiss her silly.

Adam was a great deal more cheerful on the way back to the house, where they found Huw and Rhosyn up and dressed and eager to welcome this other large playmate, who proved only too happy to keep them entertained. Tired out at last, the two excited babies had finally been settled down for the night before Adam and his mother took their leave.

'I can't tell you what this has meant to both of us,' said Adam with sincerity as he thanked Geraint and Holly.

'Adam's right,' said Mrs Hawkridge as she kissed Lowri. 'I never expected to enjoy a Christmas so much again.'

'I'll be in touch,' promised Lowri. 'You must come and see my shop and spoil Rhosyn as much as you like.'

'I'll keep you to that, my dear!'

Tactfully Geraint and Holly walked with Mrs Hawkridge to the car, leaving Adam and Lowri to say their goodbyes in private.

'When shall I see you again?' demanded Adam.

'I don't know,' she said evasively. 'Call me. We'll talk about it.'

For answer Adam swept her into his arms and kissed her hard, then took her hand and ran with her to the car waiting at the gate. After he got in he put his head out of the window and thanked the Morgans again, then gave Lowri the smile which still made her heart turn over.

'Soon!' he said and drove his mother away.

CHAPTER THIRTEEN

'How did it go?' asked Sarah a couple of days later, when Lowri was back in Pennington.

'It was a bit awkward at first,' admitted Lowri. 'I mean, the last time Dad and Adam met wasn't exactly a friendly occasion, was it? But no one could bristle in Mrs Hawkridge's company for long——'

'I told you she was lovely!'

'You were right. It was a mutual love affair between Mrs H. and Rhosyn from the first—Huw adored her, too. Under any other circumstances I might have been quite jealous. And oddly enough, once they'd got over the first hurdle Dad and Adam got on surprisingly well. Holly liked him a lot, I could tell, though she tried hard to hide it from me in case I thought she was being disloyal. Anyway, enough of me. How was your Christmas?'

'Exhausting, but fun. Though not as much fun as yours, by the sound of it. I'd love to have been a fly on the wall in Cwmderwen for the first half-hour!'

Lowri chuckled. 'Oh, by the way, did you ring Rhia?'

'I certainly did. She was horrified, needless to say, and sends loads of love; so does Mari-Sian. They'll be round to see you the moment they get back.' Sarah paused. 'So what happens now, Lowri?'

'I get back to work and life goes on, I suppose.'

'I mean what happens with Adam?'

'I'm not sure,' said Lowri guardedly. 'I can't stop him seeing Rhosyn after what happened, of course, but there's been no talk of—of arrangements, and so on.'

'Surely you've thawed a bit towards him by now?'

'Not much.'

Sarah sighed. 'You always were an obstinate little mule. Anyway, I trust you're all organised for my New Year's Eve soirée?'

'Yes. Fran's going to lock up and so on at the shop, so I'll drive down after lunch, well in time to get Rosie to bed.'

'Emily can't wait! And I'm quite looking forward to seeing you myself,' added Sarah affectionately. 'Buy a new dress. You deserve it.'

Lowri was visited with a strong feeling of *déjà vu* as she went down the curving staircase in St John's Wood to join one of the Clares' celebrated parties. She paused halfway down, suffering a sudden attack of stage-fright at the sound of laughter and music from the drawing-room, and gave herself a stern lecture. Her only problem was lack of practice these days when it came to socialising. Since Rhosyn's advent she'd had no time or opportunity for it. Tonight would do her good. Besides, she reminded herself, she'd already met several of the guests invited tonight. And the new dress she'd bought for half-price in the expensive shop just up the street from Little Darlings looked good on her, she knew. But a flattering dress and the glittering crystal earrings Holly had given her for Christmas were neither of them remedies for the butterflies fluttering beneath her green velvet midriff.

Then a familiar figure crossed the hall and looked up and Tom Harvey let out a crow of delight.

'Lowri! What a sight to gladden these old eyes. Let me ply you with strong drink and tell you how gorgeous you look.'

Suddenly Lowri was brimming with party spirit, and went running down to let Tom sweep her into the drawing-room into the crush of people gathered there to celebrate the new year. There were exclamations of pleasure from people she'd known before her flight from London, and a welcome from others meeting her for the first time. Now that her hair had grown and her rigorous diet and exercise routine had pared down her figure Lowri's likeness to Sarah was much more marked, and commented on by several people who mistook her for another sister. Rupert seized her hand to introduce her to a tall, lanky young man with a laughing intelligent face, and told him to take care of his little cousin.

'Lowri here did the donkey work for *The Atonement*,' said Rupert grinning. 'So be careful how you tread. She's a tigress in defence of my matchless prose.'

'I'm directing the adaptation for television,' the man told Lowri, as Rupert went off to welcome new arrivals. 'My name's Jack Benedict. Why haven't I met you before?'

'Because I don't live in London, I suppose.'

Jack led her to a secluded corner and began firing a barrage of questions at her, as to what she did and where she did it, whether she was spoken for and if not could he see her again as soon as possible.

Lowri, laughing, made her answers deliberately vague and settled down to indulge in the type of flirtation she'd forgotten she enjoyed so much. It was fun to talk light-hearted nonsense with a man not only expert in the art, but flatteringly determined to keep her to himself.

But after a while Lowri excused herself.

'Where are you going?' said Jack in alarm. 'It's not midnight yet, so don't vanish on me like Cinderella.'

'I'm just going upstairs to check on my daughter,' she assured him, and grinned at the crestfallen look on his face.

'So you are married,' he said, sighing theatrically.

'No, I'm not.' She handed him her glass. 'Hold on to that for me. I shan't be long.'

Lowri ran up the stairs and went along the upper hall to the guest-room she was sharing with her daughter.

She opened the door very quietly, then stared, transfixed. Adam Hawkridge, looking spectacular in formal black and white, was gazing down at his sleeping daughter, with a look on his face which flipped Lowri's heart over under the dark green velvet. He turned silently as he sensed her presence, and the thick dark brows drew together in a scowl as he seized her arm in a bruising grip and hustled her from the room.

'What the hell do you mean by leaving Rhosyn up here on her own?' he whispered furiously. 'I saw you downstairs with some man, enjoying yourself far too much to give a thought to our daughter!'

Lowri shook off his hand, incensed. 'There's an intercom on the table alongside the cot. The other half's in the next room with Dominic, who'd be down to me in a second if she woke. Besides, it's only half an hour since I left her to go downstairs. Not,' she added, shaking with rage, 'that it's any business of yours!'

'The hell it isn't!' Adam seized her by the elbows and shook her until her earrings tinkled together like windchimes. 'She's mine, too, remember.'

'Do you think I ever forget?' she spat, and at once his hands fell away and the fury drained from his face.

'So you're going to make me pay for the rest of my life,' he said dully.

Her eyes flashed. 'Certainly not. I don't want any payment from you. Ever.'

They stared at each other in silence, then Dominic shot out of his room and came to a full stop, his eyes lighting up at the sight of the tall, tense man.

'Adam—hi!' he said, 'Mum was afraid you wouldn't come.'

Adam's eyes softened as he shook Dominic's hand, then cuffed him playfully. 'What's your mother feeding you on? You're shooting up like a beanstalk.'

Dominic grinned, then frowned anxiously. 'I came out to see Rosie. She was making a bit of a noise over the intercom.'

Lowri thanked him affectionately and hurried back into the bedroom to investigate, then smiled as she heard the noise worrying Dominic. Her daughter was snoring.

The tall young teenager put a hand to his mouth to stifle his laughter as he peered over Lowri's shoulder. He turned to Adam, made a thumbs-up sign and went out, leaving the others to follow him more slowly. Outside on the landing Adam rubbed a hand over his face wearily, then looked at Lowri.

'I'm sorry. I over-reacted. Rhosyn's adventure seems to have knocked my equilibrium endwise.'

'I never neglect her,' said Lowri flatly.

'I know.' His mouth twisted. 'I was just being bloody-minded. I saw you with that guy downstairs when I arrived and I was jealous, so I lashed out in the way I knew would hurt most.'

Lowri's eyes widened. 'You were jealous?'

'Is it surprising?' His eyes moved over her slowly. 'You look so beautiful, Lowri. So poised and self-contained; I hardly recognise the girl who blushed at me over the sexy underwear.'

Lowri eyed the stairs pointedly. 'We should go down.'

'In a minute.' Adam caught her hand in his. 'Before I go tonight, Lowri, I want some kind of concession about Rhosyn. Make any reasonable rules you want and I'll stick to them religiously, I swear. But don't let her grow up thinking her father doesn't care for her.'

'No,' she said, detaching her hand. 'I won't do that. I'll work something out, I promise. Now we really must go down. I promised Sarah I'd help with supper.'

The next couple of hours went by in a blur, as Lowri laughed and flirted with Tom Harvey and the patiently waiting Jack Benedict, happy to talk about Rhosyn to Carey Savage, who was insistent she take her baby to see her before she left London. At supper Lowri helped Sarah make sure no guest lacked anything in the way of food and drink, an arrangement which allowed her a little private conversation with her cousin.

'You didn't say Adam was coming,' she accused in an undertone.

'Rupert said you'd be mad, but I think it's a good idea,' said Sarah unrepentantly. 'Time to bury the hatchet.'

'Where exactly shall I bury it?' hissed Lowri, and turned with a smile to offer strawberry *feuilleté* to Jack.

Adam spent most of the evening talking to Rupert with Patrick Savage, but every time Lowri looked up she found his eyes on her, and looked away, hoping he'd leave early so she could enjoy herself properly. Which, she told herself bitterly, was a whopping great lie. If Adam left the party would be well and truly over for her.

Just before twelve Sarah brought in a transistor radio while Rupert and Lowri handed out glasses of champagne to everyone as they gathered together for the countdown to midnight. When Lowri handed Adam his glass he seized her wrist and kept her close by his side as everyone chanted the last seconds until Big Ben struck the hour to usher in the new year. Adam thrust his glass to Lowri's lips, and she drank involuntarily, then he put the glass to his own lips and drained it and took her in his arms and kissed her.

'Happy New Year, Lowri,' he said huskily.

'Happy New Year, Adam,' she answered mechanically, her eyes locked with his, and ignoring the mêlée of jostling, kissing people about them he set down the glass and took her in his arms again, this time kissing her at such length that only applause and catcalls from an audience of laughing people brought them both back to earth.

Lowri, scarlet-faced, was seized by Rupert, then by Sarah, with much kissing and laughter, then Sarah nodded significantly at Adam.

'Go on. I've got my instructions.'

Lowri had a quick glimpse of Jack Benedict's rueful face as Adam rushed her through the hall, and then the kitchen, and out through the back door he slammed shut behind them before racing with her across the frost-crisp grass to the coachhouse, deaf to her protests.

'What do you think you're doing?' she gasped, stumbling in unaccustomed high heels.

'What I should have done a long time ago,' said Adam tersely, and dragged her unceremoniously up the familiar iron stairs to the flat and unlocked the door.

'But Rhosyn——'

'Dominic will tell Sarah if she wakes.' Adam switched on a lamp, and shut the door, jerking his head at the telephone on the desk. 'One ring from that and we can be back in the house in seconds. But for the moment——' He let out his breath slowly and released her hand. 'But for the moment I need to speak to you in peace, without any amorous editors and TV directors butting in.'

Lowri's heart began to slow down again. 'You've spoken to me several times lately,' she pointed out prosaically. 'What's so special about tonight?'

'Our previous encounters were too emotive to allow for practical discussion,' he said quietly. 'And my phone calls to enquire after Rhosyn the last couple of days were hardly productive. Your telephone manner is straight out of the deep freeze, Lowri.'

She shrugged. 'You could at least have told me you were coming here tonight.'

'I was pretty sure you wouldn't turn up if I did.'

'If I'd had any idea you intended that—that exhibition in there just now I'd have stayed at home!' she snapped, and folded her arms.

'I didn't intend anything,' he cut back. 'It just happened!' He sighed impatiently. 'Look, Lowri, I want ten minutes of your time. Then you're free. To get back to the party, or whatever else you want.'

Lowri sat down on the sofa. 'All right. Get it over with, then.'

Adam loomed over her, frowning. 'Why are you so hostile, for God's sake? After what happened to Rhosyn, and Christmas and so on, I thought you were softening towards me.'

'I was,' she retorted, 'until I found you with Rhosyn tonight, at which point your accusations sent my good intentions up in flames!'

'I've apologised for that,' he said stiffly.

'True. So what is it that's so important you have to drag me from the party to say it?'

Adam let himself down beside her warily, as if he expected her to jump up and run at any moment. 'First of all, there's something my mother thinks I should have told you from the first.'

Lowri's eyes narrowed. 'Go on.'

'During our brief but unforgettable relationship,' said Adam tonelessly, 'you may remember I was up to my ears in taking over the company from my father. And an unkind fate made you choose the worst possible day to explode your little bombshell in my ear. I'd just learned that my father had only a short time to live.'

Lowri gazed at him in horror. 'You didn't know before?'

Adam shook his head. 'No one did, except my mother. And she firmly refused to let it spoil what time they had left. Their long, lazy cruise together, Dad told me at the end, was the best preparation for heaven a man could ever wish for.'

There was silence for a moment, then he cleared his throat and went on.

'He also told me that marriage to the right woman was exactly what I needed. But by then, of course, it was too late. My one hope of that vanished the day you disappeared from my life.'

'Oh, come *on*,' said Lowri scornfully, 'If that's the case why were you so perfectly bloody to me when I told you I was pregnant?'

'At that particular moment in time it was the straw that broke the camel's back. I was dog-tired from overwork, and Dad had just let me in on a tragic secret I had to keep to myself. I was off my head with grief when you arrived that night.' Adam took her hand in a painful grip. 'I'm not proud of it, dammit, but when you told me you were pregnant I flipped. And by the time I realised what I'd done and tried to redeem myself with a proposal it was too late. You'd retreated into your little shell and I couldn't do a blind thing about it.'

'But you grew colder and more remote by the minute right up to the date we'd set for the wedding,' cried Lowri, twisting round to face him. 'Why?'

Adam stared blankly. 'What are you talking about? You were the cold, remote one, Lowri. You made me feel so bloody guilty I was afraid to touch you!'

She eyed him dubiously. 'Are you telling me the truth?'

His mouth twisted. 'Yes, Lowri, I am. And while we're on the subject there's another little detail my mother bawled me out for keeping to myself, too.'

Lowri thawed a little. 'What was that?'

Adam shrugged. 'From your point of view it might be a total irrelevance. But you may as well hear it all. When I finally realised my bride wasn't going to turn up that day something hit me right between the eyes. Not having come up against it before, it had never occurred to me—until that moment—why you were so different from the other girls I'd known.'

'You made no secret of the fact that my girlish enthusiasm for your bed appealed to you most,' she said tartly, trying to release her hand.

Adam's grip tightened. 'It was part of it,' he agreed. 'But the difference between you and all the rest was the simple fact that I loved you.'

Lowri stared at him in utter disbelief. 'Would you mind saying that again?'

'Certainly.' Adam's colour heightened slightly. 'I'll say it as many times as you like now I've started. I discovered I loved you, Lowri, and I still love you, and just to put the icing on the cake I'm pretty sure, heaven help me, that I always will love you.' He let go of her hand. 'Right. That's all I had to say. Now you can go back to the party.'

She shook her head thoughtfully. 'I don't think I will, thanks just the same.'

He moved nearer. 'Why?' he demanded. 'Is a slight change of heart possible on your part now I've come clean at last?'

She shook her head. 'No.'

His face darkened. 'None whatsoever?'

She smiled a little. 'Adam, I fell in love with you the moment I first saw you. I battled against it but it wasn't any use—no——' She warded him off. 'It's because I loved you so desperately that your reaction to my news hurt so badly.'

'And you stopped loving me from that moment on,' he said heavily, his colour receding. 'Which is why you left me waiting that day.'

'No. You're wrong,' she said matter-of-factly. 'I loved you so much, in fact, that I couldn't face the thought of marrying someone who was only doing it because he felt obliged to.'

'It was never like that,' said Adam morosely, looking away. 'I admit I suggested marriage as the only possible solution to our little problem. But I only discovered the

real reason for my proposal when it dawned on me you
weren't going to turn up. That day or any other.' He
breathed in deeply. 'If revenge was your object, Lowri,
you got it in spades. I hope it was sweet.'

'No, it wasn't,' said Lowri swiftly. 'It was you I
wanted, not revenge. I never stopped wanting you or
loving you, either, no matter how hard I tried. When I
had Rhosyn it was you I wanted with me, not Sarah or
Rhia or even Dad. Just you. That's why there's no change
of heart, Adam. I've never stopped loving you——'

Adam seized her in his arms. 'Is that the truth?' His
eyes glowed with a light so brilliant that Lowri's closed,
dazzled. She nodded dumbly, and he bent his mouth to
hers in an oddly passionless kiss.

But after a while the kiss changed, Adam's mouth
asking questions which hers answered with fervour, and
suddenly her fingers were undoing his bow tie and his
were busy with her zip, then the phone rang.

'Sorry to interrupt,' said Sarah. 'But there's a young
lady over here who needs her parents.'

'Is she crying?' demanded Lowri breathlessly, her face
scarlet.

'No. She seems to want to play. And while I'd be happy
to oblige I still have guests——'

'We'll be there right now!' Lowri put down the phone
and grinned at Adam. 'Our daughter demands our
presence.'

Adam caught her close and crushed the life out of her
with his hug. 'I never thought I'd hear you say "our".
Let's go.' He smiled ruefully as he smoothed back her
hair. 'A pity she couldn't have waited just a little longer.'

Lowri chuckled as they clattered down the iron steps.
'Welcome to fatherhood, Adam Hawkridge. Are you
sure it's what you want?'

'Positive,' he panted as they raced across the lawn.
'And I'm not really sorry we were interrupted. When I
get you in my bed at last I want you there all night.'

'You'll be lucky,' whispered Lowri, as they stole up the stairs. 'Rhosyn wakes up sometimes, remember.'

Adam stopped just outside the guest-room door. 'In which case we take turns—no more single blessedness for you, Lowri Morgan. Soon,' he added sternly, 'to be Hawkridge, I'd remind you.'

'We've got a lot of sorting out to do before then——'

'Then come and do it in here with your daughter,' said Sarah, hurrying from the room. She grinned at them both and hurried off. 'Blessings, my children,' she said over her shoulder. 'Come and have some more champagne when Rosie's settled.'

Lowri and Adam found their daughter standing up in her cot, banging the rails with her new teddy.

'Mum-mum!' she said with a wide smile, then spotted Adam. She bridled a little flirtatiously, dropped the teddy and held up her arms. He scooped her up and held her close, his eyes meeting Lowri's over her head.

'She knows me,' he said incredulously.

'She knows you're a soft touch!' said Lowri, grinning, then raised an eyebrow at a look of panic on his face. 'What's up?'

'She's a bit damp round the edges!'

Lowri's lips twitched. 'Right. You may as well start as you go on. You can change her nappy.'

Laughing uproariously at Adam's look of horror, Lowri gave him step-by-step instructions on the process, which Rhosyn proceeded to make as difficult as she possibly could, sensing an amateur. Lowri looked up with a smile as Dominic popped a tousled head round the door, brandishing the intercom speaker.

He smiled cheekily. 'I can hear every word on this, you know, so just in case you're going to get soppy I've brought it back.' He sauntered over to eye Adam's panting exertions with the wriggling baby. 'Gosh, you're not much good as a dad, are you?'

Adam looked up at Lowri with a smile of such triumph that her eyes filled. 'Not yet,' he agreed, 'and for this particular job I don't intend to be, frankly.' He picked up his daughter and tossed her in the air. 'But otherwise, all I need is practice!'

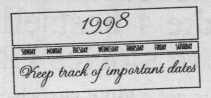

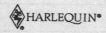

Take 4 bestselling love stories FREE
Plus get a FREE surprise gift!

Special Limited-time Offer

Mail to Harlequin Reader Service®

3010 Walden Avenue
P.O. Box 1867
Buffalo, N.Y. 14240-1867

YES! Please send me 4 free Harlequin Romance® novels and my free surprise gift. Then send me 6 brand-new novels every month, which I will receive months before they appear in bookstores. Bill me at the low price of $2.67 each plus 25¢ delivery and applicable sales tax if any*. That's the complete price and a savings of over 10% off the cover prices—quite a bargain! I understand that accepting the books and gift places me under no obligation ever to buy any books. I can always return a shipment and cancel at any time. Even if I never buy another book from Harlequin, the 4 free books and the surprise gift are mine to keep forever.

116 BPA A3UK

Name	(PLEASE PRINT)	
Address	Apt. No.	
City	State	Zip

This offer is limited to one order per household and not valid to present Harlequin Romance® subscribers. *Terms and prices are subject to change without notice. Sales tax applicable in N.Y.

UROM-696

©1990 Harlequin Enterprises Limited

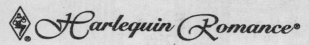

Invites You to A Wedding!

Whirlwind Weddings
Combines the heady
romance of a whirlwind
courtship with the
excitement of a wedding—
strong heroes, feisty
heroines and marriages
made not so much in
heaven as in a hurry!

What's the catch? All our heroes and heroines meet
and marry within a week! Mission impossible?
Well, a lot can happen in seven days....

January 1998—#3487 MARRY IN HASTE
by Heather Allison

February 1998—#3491 DASH TO THE ALTAR
by Ruth Jean Dale

March 1998—#3495 THE TWENTY-FOUR-HOUR BRIDE
by Day Leclaire

April 1998—#3499 MARRIED IN A MOMENT
by Jessica Steele

Who says you can't hurry love?

Available wherever Harlequin books are sold.

Free Gift Offer

With a Free Gift proof-of-purchase
from any Harlequin® book, you can receive
a beautiful cubic zirconia pendant.

This stunning marquise-shaped stone is a genuine cubic
zirconia—accented by an 18" gold tone necklace.
(Approximate retail value $19.95)

Send for yours today...
compliments of ◆ HARLEQUIN®

To receive your free gift, a cubic zirconia pendant, send us one original proof-of-purchase, photocopies not accepted, from the back of any Harlequin Romance®, Harlequin Presents®, Harlequin Temptation®, Harlequin Superromance®, Harlequin Intrigue®, Harlequin American Romance®, or Harlequin Historicals® title available at your favorite retail outlet, together with the Free Gift Certificate, plus a check or money order for $1.65 U.S./$2.15 CAN. (do not send cash) to cover postage and handling, payable to Harlequin Free Gift Offer. We will send you the specified gift. Allow 6 to 8 weeks for delivery. Offer good until December 31, 1997, or while quantities last. Offer valid in the U.S. and Canada only.

Free Gift Certificate

Name: _____

Address: _____

City: _____ State/Province: _____ Zip/Postal Code: _____

Mail this certificate, one proof-of-purchase and a check or money order for postage and handling to: HARLEQUIN FREE GIFT OFFER 1997. In the U.S.: 3010 Walden Avenue, P.O. Box 9071, Buffalo NY 14269-9057. In Canada: P.O. Box 604, Fort Erie, Ontario L2Z 5X3.

FREE GIFT OFFER
084-KEZ

ONE PROOF-OF-PURCHASE
To collect your fabulous FREE GIFT, a cubic zirconia pendant, you must include this original proof-of-purchase for each gift with the properly completed Free Gift Certificate.

084-KEZR